Wri

Thea Atkinson

Published by Thea Atkinson
Cover design by Thea Atkinson

PROLOGUE

The tears came easily enough, if Taetha pinched the girl, which was fortunate because the babe hadn't cried once since she'd been born. It was almost as though she understood what she was and harbored each droplet of water for fear someone would use it against her. Seven turns of the sun and still the infant hadn't cried. Seven turns, and still she wouldn't suckle.

What kept the babe alive, Taetha would never know, but the brown magics could be good and the power, when it was harnessed as it was in this child, was strong. No doubt the babe psyched from the very air what water she needed to sustain her, but even that couldn't keep the tiny heart beating for much longer. She needed to eat.

Taetha looked down at the narrow vial she'd lain against the infant's cheek and pinched the earlobe once more. The babe's squall leaked a few more precious tears into the glass. They were indeed precious; and precious little, barely covering the bottom, but perhaps, if The Deities were kind, it would be enough.

She plugged the vial with a knob of cork and poured beeswax around the neck to seal it, rolling it in her palm to cool. There was so little of the fluid, she couldn't take the chance of evaporation, or spilling, or worse, any psyching from it if the girl grew thirsty. She grunted in satisfaction and wrapped the tube, now cooled and hardened of its seal, into a thick hide, tied that with hare intestines dried and oiled to perfect suppleness, and then laid it in a basket lined with moss. This she covered with yet another hide and tied that with yet more hare thongs before settling the entire package near the door.

He would be coming soon.

Taetha had let the fire pit purposely die down and she glanced at it to be sure the coals were tamped. The iron poker lay where she left it beside the pit, seemingly forgotten to the casual eye, but well within easy reach should she need it.

Why she would be afraid of a child—a boy—she couldn't say, but these last months she'd learned not all was as it seemed. The brown magic could grow black if left too long unused and mouldering. She'd not dared use what she owned since she'd been taken, indeed, none of them had dared: her brother, her sister. Alhanna: their mother. But she couldn't think about them, not now. She had enough to concern her with the boy's visit.

With magics becoming a liability, and black magic rising from brown, she worried the boy had been left too long with the darkness—or worse—counselled in darkness and had been spoiled before his life had ripened. The klans had warred too long to know if one witch or more had gone to seed, the reason for their fighting long forgotten. She only knew this babe needed her, and she no longer cared for the old war. Truth be told, the old war mattered little now that the Conqueror had come, mattered little in light of the need to band together against this common enemy. Perhaps this child would help heal the rift among the klans and bring them together finally; this self-proclaimed conqueror making them forget the old hatreds.

The infant whimpered and Taetha eased her from the basket where she lay and pulled her close against her chest, letting the scent of new flesh envelope her and make her feel again the lingering magics of her home and its tribe. It seemed she couldn't leave it all behind, after all. Well, she could ignore the old war, but she could not ignore the heritage.

"Shall I sing to you of Etlantium, Little One," she said to the fuzz of hair. "Or should your nohma tell you once again of your mother?"

She hummed, letting the babe nestle into her neck. How warm the girl was. How tiny to fit into such close places as a matron's neck, an arm's crook, a heart that had seized up over the last days into a tiny knot of flesh.

So small, but so, so powerful. Would this boy guess the power he was being bonded to? Would his mother?

She was still humming when the fire pit leapt to flame. Taetha eyed the poker and edged closer to it, turning even as she did so to the visitor she knew was standing in the door.

He was small but already had a few markings in the old language on his ribs. The first one, the largest, was easy to decipher even from her distance, as it was still inflamed at its edges: that of fire.

"You are Yenic," she said.

The boy's eyes glowed yellow, sparking in reflection of the flame.

"You are Taetha?" His voice was querulous but strong. He would be a force, this one. Taetha tried to believe the wriggling in her belly was from nervous excitement, not anxiety. The two could so often be mistaken, being as close as they were.

She drew to her full height and nodded at the basket.

"I am Taetha," she confirmed. "Blood witch to the newborn temptress." She gave him a direct look. "You were not followed." She could have phrased it as a question, but chose instead the command. Let him feel nervous.

He shook his head, unaffected, but peered over his shoulder into the garden. "I thought I was, but he proved to be only a poor drunkard pissing in the wrong spot."

Taetha said nothing. She knew the man was dead. She'd have to bury him later. This boy was indeed a child, but already his tattaus carried the weight of his mother's power. He would have been instructed to take no chances. She eyed the boy again and was relieved — even emboldened — when she saw a look of regret on his features.

"How many seasons have you, Yenic?"

"Seven."

"Seven is young to be an Arm."

He toed the dirt. "It's young to be bonded."

"You'd rather the first but not the last?"

A grin pulled at the corner of his mouth. "I'd rather it was neither."

"I understand." He was so young, yet something in his eyes made him seem far older than seven seasons. She couldn't concern herself with his woes. She had a babe to think of. She glanced toward the door.

"The basket is there." Taetha pulled the infant closer, putting her palm over the tiny head of black fuzz. "Take care travelling it."

Yenic took the few short steps to where the wicker sat bundled in hides she'd tanned and beaten with her own hand. He pulled fiercely at the thongs.

"No," she said, taking an alarmed step; she couldn't have him breaking the vial just to satisfy himself she'd given what she'd offered. "It's there. I promise you. Safe and sound."

He glanced up sharply, curious. "Oh, I know it is," he said matter-of-factly, and bent again to the hide. He pulled the vial loose, scraped at the wax and yanked the cork with his teeth. Peering at the liquid, he made a face, then spat the cork to the earthen floor where it spun twice before stopping.

"I'm not to take chances," he said as though he were repeating solemn words that he'd practiced, then upended the vial into his gaping mouth. He swallowed. He grimaced. Sighed. With an odd quirk to his lips, he looked up at Taetha. He looked far younger in the moment than the seven he was.

"It's done, isn't it?" he asked.

She felt for a telltale quickening in her chest, the echo of one fluttering against her own, and when she knew it was there, she closed her eyes in relief.

She didn't have to look to know he was gone, but she opened her eyes anyway. The door stood open and empty. The fire pit died again to its blackness.

The babe in her arms began to suckle at her neck noisily.

"It's done, Alaysha," she said to the room. "It's done, and I pray to The Deities I've done the right thing."

CHAPTER 1

Yenic's hands traveled her skin in such delicious ways that Alaysha thought she was little more than a large pheasant being seasoned with dry herbs and honey. The scent of his flesh, like so many spices drying on hot embers intoxicated her to the point she felt drugged. She stretched to enjoy the softness of his hands stroking her inner thighs, the place just beneath her navel where her skin was the most sensitive. She arched against him, taking his mouth with hers, teasing his tongue, worrying his lip with her teeth.

She tasted his moan even as she wondered if the sound came from her own lips. She fell into the amber of his eyes. Yes. Honey. So much amber liquid a girl could drown in it if she wasn't careful. She wanted to tell him how much she wanted him, how badly she needed to feel him cover her with his body, to obliterate the nakedness that made her feel vulnerable and lonely. No words would form. Only mewling sounds and heavy breaths that seemed to come from somewhere just short of her chest, that seemed too rushed to have come from anywhere deeper.

His gaze pinned her where she lay, the most aching look of sadness she'd ever seen, and she wanted to pull him down again to her, to tell him grief had no place here. When her body went cold, she realized he was fading from her, substance turned to smoke, and then smoke turned to air, and air to fragrance that had nothing to do with the youth and everything to do with a hunger far more primal.

She woke to the smell of goat's milk, and she remembered. It was a foggy remembrance, for certain, with echoes of images long buried and not understood fully even then, but still, she remembered them. They were sweeter than the dream of Yenic because as she came to consciousness, she remembered her lover could not be trusted.

The other memories, the ones that didn't carry the bittersweet bite of Yenic's betrayal — his outright lies to her — were safer ones to focus on. They felt like honey in her veins, so much so that she didn't want to open her eyes and ruin the feeling of sinking down in warm syrup.

"Are you hungry?"

The voice, a woman's, came from her right. Alaysha turned to it and opened one eye.

"I must be," she said in answer to Yuri's young wife who hovered near her elbow. The woman gave her a queer look, and Alaysha licked her lips. "I can taste goat's milk. My stomach must be sending my mouth some kind of message."

The girl chuckled. "That was me. I dribbled some of Kiki's milk onto your lips while you slept."

"You couldn't wait for me to wake up to do that?"

The woman lifted a thin shoulder. "You've been asleep six turns of the sun." The mist colored eyes retreated from view as the woman straightened to her full height. Alaysha felt oddly small beneath it. She'd forgotten how tall Yuri's new wife was. "Yuri told me to make sure you were nourished so you would wake strong."

Six turns. Six turns was a long time to be asleep, especially when it felt like mere hours.

"Kiki is your goat?" she asked the woman.

"Yes. The only one nursing. She's a new mother so her milk is sweet."

Alaysha let her tongue roam over her lips. "You make sure she eats clover too."

"How did you know that?"

Alaysha would have smiled if the memory wasn't so bittersweet.

"My nohma's goat ate clover."

She touched the corner of her mouth thoughtfully. The spring feed was always clover. Fall left nothing but bitter grass and the unending sourness of the goat's milk always made Alaysha's stomach upset then. She hadn't thought of that in years.

"There was honey in it too," she guessed, and the young woman smiled.

"I warmed the milk with honey so it would make your body too sweet for the green death." Her gaze fleeted over the bed and rested where Alaysha's stomach was. "It was a bad place for a wound. I fear even the balsam sap the shaman used won't be enough to keep it clean."

"I had fever?"

The woman nodded.

Alaysha thought for a moment. "I called out for milk."

"Yes." The wife lowered her gaze, letting her silver hair hang in her face. "You suckled on the cloth as though it were a nipple."

Alaysha felt her face suffuse with blood. She remembered. She remembered much. Goat's milk and honey. Very much like her first meal, served very much in the same manner. Her mother's sister wasn't a wet nurse, only a blood witch, and no other woman in the village would come near the infant powerhouse. None that did dare lived. That she remembered, if reluctantly.

"Six turns?" Alaysha still couldn't believe it.

"Yes. But fevered for only two. You've been sleeping comfortably for the last few hours."

Alaysha wasn't sure if that was a blessing or not. "Were there any deaths?" She wasn't sure she wanted the answer, but needed to ask.

The wife grinned and looked incredibly beautiful in that moment. She was a willowy thing; what Alaysha had presumed as frailty before, now proved to be nothing more than slender height. "Not one," the woman said. "It's almost as though you weren't here."

Her face fell when she realized what she'd said, and she stammered, trying to retract what she'd said. "I mean—"

Alaysha had to interrupt her. "It's all right. I know what you mean."

She tried to roll onto her side; her bum felt as though it was on fire. "It's not as though the village is exactly safe when its witch is burning alive."

She winced when a pain shot up her stomach, and she fell back onto her back, defeated.

The woman noticed and touched Alaysha's forehead lightly. "It's only the pain of wasting; you haven't used those muscles for so long, they are angry at being called to service."

"It feels like the last service they were called to nearly rent me in two."

Yuri's wife licked her lips in thought. "It very nearly did." Then she paused, thinking. "To be honest, I was worried at first."

Alaysha looked up at her. "Yes?"

The woman nodded. "Yes, but when I watched you very closely, I noticed any sweat you released quickly got evaporated again—as though you were pulling it back in. You didn't even make water."

"Strange," Alaysha murmured, not thinking it so at all.

"Strange, yes, but I think it is this that saved us in the end." The wife lifted a wooden bucket with some triumph. "I kept it next to your bed."

"A bucket?"

"This and a few others, filled with water. We had to refill them dozens of times on the first days. My brother and I, anyway. It took too many trips for just one of us to keep up."

Alaysha could imagine.

"It was a dozen buckets at first, all lined up next to the bed. Then half. Then two and one. The same one has been here, full, for a few hours now."

"I'm surprised you dared stay."

"Yuri sent me away during the first day of your fever. Gael and I merely lugged water."

Alaysha tried not to show surprise. "My father? My father stayed with me?" She tried to make it sound uninterested; she knew the connection of their blood would have made him the only one able to withstand her fever and its need for fluid, but knowing he'd been by her bedside during the worst gave her a strange feeling in her chest. She tried not to read any more into it than a man safeguarding one of his finest tools, but she wanted to believe it was more.

"You said you and Gael lugged water?"

"My brother."

"And Yuri sent you away?"

The wife nodded. "He said you are too dangerous."

"I imagine I was."

Alaysha didn't enjoy the feeling, but she knew it to be true. Still, she wanted to stress that danger from her was in the past tense and there was no more to fear from her. Not if she could help it.

"What of Aedus? Has she returned?" It was a jolt, remembering the girl she had worked so hard to save from the hands of her own brother, who was willing to sacrifice her and any others to get control of Sarum, knowing that same girl had gone off to ultimate danger again anyway.

The woman turned away and made a great show of arranging the bucket next to Alaysha's bed without spilling any water.

Alaysha had to press again. "Aedus? She should have returned by now."

"They returned," the woman hedged.

They. Alaysha's stomach churned thinking about the name she didn't want to mention. Yenic. She thought of her dream and felt her face burn. She tried to tell herself it was the intimacy of the vision that made her blush, not the shame of feeling used by the youth she trusted and came to care so deeply for. No. That last was not the reason for the flush of embarrassment. It couldn't be. She'd been trained too well by her father to care about anyone or to care about what anyone thought of her. Yenic might well be a traitor to her, if her father was right, but she'd wait and watch, and decide for herself. She'd use that tool her father had best given her: her stoic ability to do her duty without thinking or feeling.

Still, she had to work at sounding casual when she spoke, hard as it was to do so with the memory of Yenic's honeyed gaze lingering at the edge of her thoughts.

"So they are here in Sarum."

"No. They returned empty-handed. Yuri sent them back out this morning."

Empty-handed. That meant no Edulph. It was the reason they left—to capture the man who'd put the entire city at risk. The man who'd cut off Aedus's finger in order to bully Alaysha into agreeing to kill everyone within Sarum's walls, unless his people were let free. Aedus's own brother.

"I'm sure Yuri was pleased enough to send Yenic back out to search for him."

Alaysha noted the strange way the young wife looked at her. Obviously the sour tone had escaped through her voice after all. "My father doesn't trust Yenic." She tried, in way of explanation, but the girl's smoky brow just lifted in casual disbelief.

"Your father trusts no one and does what is best for Sarum." The young wife argued. "The two did not return with Edulph's head as they were ordered. They returned instead with a woman."

Alaysha remembered Yuri's 'orders' had been countered by Yenic when they argued about bringing this other woman to Sarum, so she knew who the woman was that the young wife spoke of without needing to ask. Yenic's mother.

Edulph himself had been lucky enough to escape Yuri's wrath when Aedus painted her brother with dreamer's worm, sending him mad with hallucinations out into the forests. Even as that small battle had been won, another larger one loomed heavy on the horizon, one that involved both Edulph and Yenic's mother.

There would be war if Yuri was right. That war would be of men trying to gain control of more than a mere city, but also of the elements. He had told her he'd wanted to avoid that, using her throughout her life to eliminate that concern by killing all of the other temptresses: those of fire and earth and air; in effect, leaving him the sole owner of the one witch who had power over water.

Not done for philanthropic desires. Oh, no. Not Yuri, Conqueror of Hordes. He had other motives. Simple. Honest. Greedy motives.

What did it matter that he couldn't control fire or air or earth, when he could manipulate the one person who could drain the fluid from any living thing? He'd been content with that victory, thinking the others were gone, until he discovered he'd not eliminated them, merely assassinated the old matrons. Two younger ones lived still, filled with the passed-down energy that enabled them to control the wind and flame. One was Yenic's mother. The other was lost to them: a babe powerful enough to harness the wind but lacking control, a witch like Alaysha, powerful but ignorant and in need of teaching.

Now, though, Yuri wasn't the only one to know about the witches. Edulph knew. And he was out there hunting for that youngest one while a woman Yuri couldn't control, a woman full grown to her power, resided within his city walls. She could imagine how fretful her father would be at that. She almost smiled, until she recalled that Yuri had reluctantly agreed to let Yenic bring his mother to Sarum under the pretense of teaching Alaysha to control her power. She wanted that desperately, even if the teacher was the woman Yenic protected despite his letting her believe differently. Yenic's mother: the witch of flame. A woman powerful enough to bring lightening to a man's skin. She felt a sudden panic thinking about that kind of control.

"She hasn't been to see me, has she?" Surely her father wouldn't allow another powerful woman to see his own witch cut down so, and helpless. "Yuri hasn't let her in here, has he?"

The wife poked at the fire absently. "Yuri has not been here since she arrived."

The wife smoothed her linen dress down against her hips and untied then retied the laces as though to unknot some problem bothering her. In a moment, she took a breath and strode to the fireplace.

"So, she hasn't seen me?"

"She has been with Yuri."

"Yes. And Yuri has not come, so she has not come." Why wouldn't the woman just say so? Why did Alaysha have to work to get such simple information? It was wearying.

"Saxa?" she said, running through her memory to find the name. "Saxa is it?" She waited for the woman to nod. "Saxa, tell me no one but you and my father have seen me like this."

"Gael."

"Gael?"

"Gael has seen you. He and I and Yuri. Theron the shaman. No more."

That was good. Alaysha wasn't sure why, but she couldn't stand the thought that the woman who controlled Yenic—who ultimately owned him—would see her helpless. She sighed in relief, and only when her own doubts were gone did she notice Saxa hadn't stopped poking at the fire.

"You're afraid," she said, realizing it.

Saxa turned to her. "She's beautiful."

Alaysha looked Saxa over, took in the willowy frame, the long plait of mist colored hair, the eyes the color of a sword edge, and tried to imagine any woman more beautiful. She found she couldn't.

"You have nothing to fear from another woman."

Saxa chortled. "I didn't fear the violence done to me by my father. I did not fear the birth bed." She dropped the poker. "I do not fear. I accept."

If it was acceptance Alaysha saw in the woman's eyes, then Alaysha didn't understand fear at all. "What is there to accept, Saxa? You're mother to the heir. He has named only one."

Alaysha couldn't say why she was even talking about this. What did she care who Yuri bedded or how they felt about it? She cared only that she get better. Learned to harness her power. She couldn't afford to care about any more people. Caring about people got them in trouble. Caring for others came at a cost she didn't want to pay.

Saxa seemed to understand. She smoothed the ruddy madder color of her homespun linen shift again then squared her shoulders.

"Yuri will want to know you're awake. I'll send Gael to him. Would you like some broth?"

Alaysha thought about it. She expected a gurgling in her belly that would warn her of hunger, but she felt nothing. Still. She must eat to gain strength. She couldn't afford to be caught here weakened.

"I'll have broth," she told Saxa. "And a leg of whatever meat you have. And… ale," she said.

Saxa grinned. "You'll have broth." She turned on her heel and went to the door where she shouted out into the yard. Moments later Alaysha saw a blonde head bow beneath the doorframe and straighten into a large man with biceps the size of a lamb's haunch.

"This is Gael," Saxa said.

Gael had to be at least as many hands high as Barruch. He wore his hair plaited, but most of that had come loose and stuck out in sprigs; the stubble on his jaw proved he hadn't pulled a blade over it in several days.

Even so, he was the most beautiful man Alaysha had ever seen.

She tried and failed to sit up, but at least she managed to keep the pain of doing so from stealing her face.

Gael offered a half smile that surprised her until he spoke; she could easily recognize the disdain in his tone. "Does it hurt, Witch?"

Alaysha thought she could happily psyche the water from him in that instant.

Saxa interrupted. "Gael, Yuri will want to know she's awake."

"Of course he will." Gael didn't move, merely raked his gaze over Alaysha's form as she worked to pull herself up. The grin on his face moved only slightly as she floundered against the pillows.

"Gael?" Saxa put her hand on his arm. "Go."

When he left, she turned to Alaysha. "I see I must ask forgiveness for my brother. He wasn't overly pleased to be called to the service of water lugging."

Alaysha thought it was probably more than that, but that Saxa was being kind. Alaysha found she couldn't meet the woman's eyes. She mumbled instead to the fur that covered the bed and that had crept up, leaving her feet bare. "No need. I'm used to it." She eased herself back finally, giving up on the struggle to sit upright.

"It's too soon," Saxa said, seeing her defeat. "You're not strong enough to sit. After some broth maybe."

"And a leg of meat."

Saxa's hands went to the fur and pulled it over Alaysha's toes. "Broth. No more until I can be sure you won't pull out the threading."

"I haven't vomited since I was a babe," Alaysha said.

"Nor worn shoes, it seems." Saxa strode to the fireplace and reached for the ladle hanging on a peg. "Your feet are calloused and filthy. I had a chore to clean the toenails."

"I prefer to be barefoot." She refused to admit the times she'd stubbed her toes on stray roots or jammed a sharp stone into her heel.

"So I see." Saxa dipped the ladle into the pot hanging over the lowest part of the fire, then emptied it into a wooden bowl. She tested it by raising the bowl to the edge of her mouth. With a nod of satisfaction, she carried it back to the bed, a wooden spoon in her other hand.

"It's not too hot," she said.

"What is it?"

"Lamb. Some wild carrots. A threshing of black rice. My own mix of herbs. Some honey." She peered down at Alaysha with what looked like mischief in her smoky eyes. "But you get only the broth." She put one hand behind Alaysha's neck and eased her head forward enough to tilt the spoonful of soup in.

It tasted divine.

And when it hit Alaysha's stomach she immediately felt suffused with heat. She clamped her mouth closed so fast on the nausea she heard her teeth clack together.

"It seems as though this is a day of firsts." Saxa's dry tone was the only thing that gave Alaysha the strength to keep the broth in. It was several moments before she could shake her head to refuse a second spoonful.

Saxa was adamant nonetheless. "You will eat this entire bowlful, Alaysha."

Alaysha jiggled her head back and forth.

"Yes, you will. Spoon by spoon. It might take hours, but you will do it."

Alaysha eyed the spoon and Saxa made a moue of frustration. "Then you will have that leg of lamb you asked for and a mug of ale." She laughed outright then. "You warriors. So strong of mind except in the face of sickness." She scooped another dribble of broth from the bowl. "More soup, or would you like that leg of lamb?"

Alaysha squeezed her eyes closed and willed her stomach quiet. It didn't exactly obey, but it didn't outright rebel. She nodded and opened her mouth slowly.

It was torturous going, but by the time she had emptied the bowl—it turned out it was only six spoonfuls—Alaysha felt strong enough to have Saxa ease her to a semi reclined position against a back of barley pillows. She thought she could smell lavender.

"It strengthens the spleen," Saxa said when she mentioned it. "I have it sewn into all our pillows."

Alaysha wasn't sure what a spleen was or why it needed strengthening, but it was pleasant to have the tang of scent drift to her nostrils when she moved, even slightly.

"Where is the heir?"

Saxa gave her clouded look. "He sleeps in the nursery."

"Yuri didn't want him near me," Alaysha guessed. She scanned the cottage and noticed the cradle was gone. The place it had rested when she was first brought in was painfully devoid of infant like items. There was even a layer of dust as though Saxa refused to walk into the space. "How long has he been away from you?"

Saxa looked up sharply. "I see him everyday. I feed him. Nurse him. Theron sees to him when I'm not there. He just isn't allowed –"

"Near me," Alaysha finished. "But you are."

The young woman's face softened. "You're wrong to think that. I volunteered, Alaysha. Yuri isn't asking me to do something because he believes I'm expendable. He allows me to be here only because I agree to keep Saxon away."

It was odd for a boy in Yuri's tribe to be named for its mother. Alaysha was surprised he allowed it. "Saxon? Son of Saxa? Why not Yuron, son of Yuri?"

"My mother's people," was all the woman said for a time, and Alaysha had to prod her.

Saxa pursed her lips as though she didn't want to answer, then said, "Few of them survived the conquest, few enough that most of them are all gone now, but we still keep the traditions, what of them we can, alive."

Alaysha couldn't imagine the great Yuri allowing his son to be named for a woman, and a frail, willowy thing like Saxa at that. "What did you do that made Yuri bow to such an unusual request?"

"Tears have magic," she said.

Of course. Alaysha would have expected no less from a woman. Resorting to tears was sometimes too often a handy tool. She'd not been allowed often to the Keep or the Court, but she'd watched people in the courtyard plenty enough when she wasn't killing for her father, and managed to sneak through the walls, a veil over the lower part of her face, or a hood pulled tight so the good people of Sarum wouldn't see the tattau. Many a man had been bested by a quiet tear. Still, the small bit of esteem she felt for the woman began to wane and she couldn't keep the scorn from her tone.

"So you wept?"

Alaysha was surprised when Saxa chuckled instead of reacting with hurt at the insult.

"The magic works both ways, dear witch." She patted Alaysha's cheek. "It was not I who shed the tears, but Yuri."

Alaysha looked Saxa over as she toddled about the cottage, setting fresh bowls on the table and pulling a pottle from a trap door in the far corner. From it she poured viscous brown ale into a tankard that she set on the table next to the bowl.

"Why aren't you in the Keep?" Alaysha asked and Saxa paused thoughtfully. She stared down at the table she'd set and finally offered Alaysha a shrug with her answer as though it was an obvious response.

"I'm here because I want to be here. I asked Yuri for my own floor. He gave it to me."

"Makes it difficult to be his Emiri."

"I have no intention of helping him rule the city."

"But the heir —"

"Saxon will learn, but he will be formed with the understanding of harmony first. Not fear. Not hard duty. He will know the way of the people his father conquered and be all the better for it."

It sounded as though Saxa had been watching Yuri for long enough to understand his cold way of rule. "And Yuri agrees to this?"

Again, that shrewd smile, both coy and knowing at the same time. Alaysha began to understand how Yuri might be managed by a woman such as Saxa. She looked delicate, but beneath was a strength that reminded Alaysha of a slender branch in the wind.

A noise caught her attention and she knew then that several men were outside. Gael entered first, ducking his head and scanning the room quickly. He nodded to the doorframe behind him and Yuri strode in. He wore the Circlet of Conquest atop his white hair, and he took it off and gripped it, the thick fingers tapping the points. He wasted no time on Alaysha, but moved to pull Saxa against him and bury his nose in her hair.

"You smell of stew and garlic."

Saxa pulled away. "I've made your favorite."

He strode to the hearth and peered in the pot. "Lamb," he said.

"Lamb stew to be exact. Black rice. No potatoes."

"Bodicca puts too many of the damned things in."

Saxa grinned with pleasure, making her eyes crinkle. "I have fresh bread too. Come this morning from the ovens." She spread her arm toward the table and nodded at Gael who pulled the chair for Yuri.

Alaysha had the feeling she was no more than a spirit in the room; no one so much as looked her way. While it was nothing new, she had expected Yuri to come see her, not just to eat a humble stew that Bodicca could have made far more substantial with all the rights she had to Yuri's kitchen. Alaysha thought of the gargantuan woman, who was the only one Yuri trusted to cook for him, the woman who had killed as many men as any other of his warriors, and she smiled. Aedus had bested the warrior woman with feet as fleet as a ferret's. She could smell honeyed hare even now, feel the stickiness of it on her fingers as Aedus had passed it to her, their stolen fare from Bodicca's fire. It seemed so long ago now.

For a time the only sound was of the three scraping bowls and smacking on bread. Alaysha's stomach gurgled and she realized the bit of broth she'd eaten had given her enough strength to realize she had an appetite. Once her stomach growled so loudly she thought she saw her father pause in dipping his bread into his bowl, but then Gael passed him the pottle of ale and they went on eating. No one looked her way.

She had time to watch them, even though Yuri's broad back was turned her. It was a torturous thing to be present in a room, and not to be included. She watched as her father touched Saxa's hand time and again, as he flicked her plait from her shoulders when it fell forward. Alaysha thought it tiring.

"Has the bucket gone dry again?" Yuri asked as though it was a logical train of conversation when nothing had been mentioned at all for long moments.

Gael nodded toward Alaysha and her heart fluttered with the hope of being noticed. "There it sits," he said.

Saxa put her hand on Yuri's arm. "Full."

Yuri nodded in appreciation even as Gael sent a scathing look toward the bed. "She had me fetching a dozen times a day, not to mention Saxa."

Alaysha thought she heard Yuri chuckle. "You can be grateful you were able to keep fetching then."

He pushed away from the table, finally; the brother and sister both eased up as well. "Good, then. It's time enough." He leaned to kiss Saxa on the forehead. "You can have Saxon after three more moon rises," he said and nodded imperially at Gael. "Take the witch to the yard today."

Gael scowled but said nothing.

Alaysha's heart dropped. It seemed Yuri had come all this way just to ignore her. She should have known. Still, she couldn't help trying.

"Father?"

Yuri turned to her as though he hadn't known she was even there. His eyes from across the distance could have been grey, not the lake water blue she knew they were. She knew he didn't like the use of the title, but he didn't correct her like he usually did.

"I would like to meet the other witch."

He shook his head. "You are too weak yet; you've lain here too long." His attention went again to Gael. "Get her ready," he said, then he strode to the door without so much as a glance back over his shoulder.

"That went well," Saxa said, beaming after he'd left as though she'd won some game, but Gael kept his scowl and prowled about the room with such conviction Alaysha wondered why he'd bothered lugging the water for her in the first place. Saxa finally growled at him to keep still; he plopped himself on the stool by the now-dying fire and waved irritably toward the bed.

"How am I to get her up and about?" His tone revealed his annoyance. "She's useless. Can't even sit up properly."

Alaysha shifted subtly against the pillow. "I can hear you." She complained, hoping the two of them would include her but was rewarded with no more than a shrug from the wide shoulders.

"I have better things to do than play nursemaid."

Saxa's comment to her brother was nearly a whisper, but Alaysha heard it just the same. "You aren't a nursemaid, brother; that's my role. You are rehabilitator—a far grander—and far more dangerous duty."

He made his lips rattle together in disgust. "Dangerous," he scoffed. "You overestimate the girl's power."

"It's not her power I speak of," Saxa said, and Alaysha understood even if Gael didn't that if she failed to regain her strength and recover suitably enough for her father, Gael's life would be forfeit.

CHAPTER 2

It took a bit of doing, a lot of cursing, and a full bowl of soup for Alaysha to finally stand. When she did, it was shortly after vomiting an entire bowl of broth onto Gael's feet, and she looked up at him carefully, knowing the sweat was beading on her forehead.

"I haven't vomited since I was a babe," she said by way of explanation.

"Then it seems you've selected an equally infantile moment and manner to do so again." He lifted his nose to the air while Saxa hurried to cleanse his boots of sour lamb chunks.

"It's too soon," Saxa worried. "You won't even make it to the door."

"I'll make it," Alaysha said and she thought she heard a low hum come from Gael's chest.

"Stop coddling her," he told his sister.

Alaysha felt bolstered enough to take a wobbling step. The accompanying pain in her side took the breath from her lungs.

Gael glanced down at her. "I've got you," he said, and Alaysha let the water in her legs ooze to the floor. She would have fallen, except Gael did indeed have her. Just being able to let her strength go for a moment gave her back her lungs.

"I can do it," she said and kept her gaze hard on Saxa's face. The smoky brows were scuttled down in concern, but at least the face wasn't terrified. Rather, it spoke of cautious confidence.

Alaysha took another step. The pain still shrieked its existence, but at least she was prepared for it and kept her legs. The wooziness was another tale entirely, and she determined that she would take a step and another until she had convinced them she wasn't worthless. Even as she thought it, she found herself wondering why she cared.

Gael took a step toward the table, and Alaysha took one, carefully, with him. It was odd not to have her body do exactly as she willed without extreme effort. She would have been discouraged by all the energy it took just to make such small, insignificant steps, but she wouldn't show weakness in front of this condescending man or the woman who had shown her kindness despite the very real danger to her that she'd undoubtedly faced each day while Alaysha was under fever.

She sweated and she cursed, and eventually she made it to the table, where Saxa had a tankard of spiced and honeyed ale, cooled by the earth storage of the food pit.

Nothing had ever tasted so good. She even shot a grin at Gael who grinned back, however fleetingly.

"Get me some of that stew, Saxa," she declared when she saw the smile slink from Gael's face, "I feel like chewing on some meat."

To her surprise, it was Gael who strode to the pot and spooned out four lumps of meat then grabbed for a trencher of bread.

"Here." He thrust it at her, then made for the bucket next to the bed and brought it close to the table within easy reach for her. "When you're done, we'll make our way to the well."

He gave her a queer look before striding to the door.

The meat was tender and delicious, with a stewed-in flavour that sat on the back of Alaysha's palette.

"What spice did you use?" she asked Saxa. "It's hot but sweet at the same time."

Saxa looked pleased. "Herbs. And it's two. The first one lingers but a moment and introduces you to the second. That's the one you taste now. I call it the bottom. It grows on the edge of the mountain on the shady side."

"And the first?"

"I call it the greeter."

"I've not tasted either before." Alaysha didn't want to admit she'd not tasted many things beyond what she could find or scavenge.

Saxa chuckled. "I discovered they have useful properties beside taste; although I keep those to myself."

Something tingled up Alaysha's spine.

"How do you feel?" Saxa asked with a note behind her voice that spoke of mild curiosity.

Alaysha chewed thoughtfully. "Kind of warm, but in a good way."

Saxa's gaze went to the table, but not before Alaysha saw something in it that raised her suspicion. "Would Yuri feel the same after his meal?"

Saxa pulled a stool close and sat on it. She took Alaysha's hand. "No. He would feel very differently, but it's not a bad thing. There's no poison."

"Then why do I feel so..."

"Tingly?"

Alaysha nodded and Saxa put three fingers against her heart as she spoke. "The greeter opens the pathways from here."

"And the bottom?"

"There's the secret," Saxa said, "The bottom carries nourishment from there to every part of your body straight to the toes."

"Then why would Yuri feel different than me?"

"Yuri's pathways do not carry his blood so well anymore. It's possible he merely feels normal."

Alaysha could feel the confusion puddling in.

"Are you saying my father is ill?"

"I'm saying he would be ill."

"If you weren't feeding him this elixir of medicine," Alaysha guessed.

"Theron has told me Yuri's heart is weak."

"Theron?"

"The shaman. He tends to Yuri with his drafts, and I tend to him with mine." Saxa shrugged. "Who knows which is helping or hurting, but until I can find a medicine to strengthen his heart, this potion will have to do. He has no idea. He just believes I am a better cook than Bodicca."

Alaysha thought of the giant of a woman who did all of Yuri's food preparation on campaign. She pictured the twist of men's teeth around the woman's forearm and the way she coddled Yuri with the most succulent of meals. Yuri trusted no one else to prepare food for him—except, obviously, Saxa. She found it interesting that the only other cook he trusted was actually drugging him without his knowledge, and that the drug was very possibly keeping him alive.

"Gael, too, ate of the stew," she said.

"Gael will feel invigorated like you do." Saxa got up and took Alaysha by the arm. "And since it seems you will not vomit out any more of my medicine, I shall help you to the well."

It wasn't an easy task to rise again, but Alaysha did feel as though her legs were more solid than a swelling river eroding its banks. She took to her feet without swaying and her stomach didn't churn at the feel of meat within. She met Saxa's eyes and nodded encouragingly.

Gael stood beside the well, when they'd made it that far, seeming oblivious to the dozens of chickens rooting about his feet or the line of young girls come to draw water.

Alaysha noticed the pile of bodies that had been there half a fortnight earlier, during Edulph's planned attack on Sarum, had been cleared and that the platform was loaded again with archers. They were dressed oddly for a Sarum collection, with motley tunics and filthy breeks. For a second, a flash of memory came to her and threatened to overtake the hard work of walking so far, and she had to gulp for air.

Saxa's voice grounded her. "Do you feel well?"

Alaysha nodded weakly.

"It's only your body remembering its insult."

Insult was a weak word for what had been done to it by her father's lead scout bent on killing her, and with the curse of power came that curse of long memory it brought. She could easily imagine Drahl dancing in front of her again, his sword wet with blood, the water from the well rising in mist to quench the fire of pain in her belly. Alaysha had to swallow hard to remind herself that fear was not part of a warrior's code. That she needn't fear that which was already done and survived.

"I'm not sure my body will ever let me forget," she said. "I just hope it hurts less each time I remember."

Saxa stopped within feet of the well and twisted so her face was in full view. "I can help with that."

"With the pain or the memory?"

"Both."

Alaysha threw a glance at Gael who had crossed his arms to indicate his impatience.

"How do you know so much?" Alaysha asked. "And how much does he know?"

Saxa looked over her shoulder at Gael. "He has the gift of war. I have the gift of peace." She shrugged. "I just know, Alaysha. Don't ask how. My father wanted to know the same thing, and I couldn't answer." Her fingers were on Alaysha's hair and she felt her forehead swept clean. "It's why he beat me."

Alaysha didn't know what to say at such a forthright and emotionless admission, and when Saxa's face brightened and her tone shifted to a more conversational one, any chance of saying more was gone.

"Don't let him work you too hard, Alaysha, he's a bear for duty." Saxa left with a pat on Alaysha's back and a promise of a brew to help with what ailed her.

It seemed she would have to make the last few steps to Gael by herself. He neither put out a hand, nor took a step forward. His eyes, so much like his sister's, were inscrutable. Alaysha easily recognized the battle training of steely composure and knew he, at least, wouldn't laugh if she fell.

She tried a step and found if she kept her eyes on his, she could make it without feeling too much pain. She took another. Another. She was nearly to him when she felt a great thud from the side. A slice of burning pain shot up from the healing wound into her throat. It was all she could do not to cry out.

She landed on the ground, her cheek against the cool dirt, her knees drawn up to her stomach before she could stop herself. She decided, in light of the pain, that lying there might just be her best option.

"Get up."

She felt a boot tip in her ribs.

She hadn't realized her eyes were closed, but when she opened them, she saw Gael's face in front of hers. His eyes weren't smoky, she realized. They were green, outlined with brown. Peculiar. And stunning.

"I told you to get up."

She might speak to defend herself if she wasn't biting her tongue to keep from crying. He sighed and his face spoke of frustration and impatience. She had the unnerving thought that he would kick her. Maybe he had kicked her.

"You pushed me," she managed to say.

He gave her a dry look. "It was a boy. No more than three seasons who pushed you."

His tone implied she was weak.

"I have been injured, you know," she said in her defence and wasn't sure she liked the sulky sound in her own voice.

He appeared unaffected. "Many get injured. Many die; some live. You are lucky."

She groaned because she knew he was right. "I know," she said. "Get up."

He folded his arms across his broad chest and Alaysha found herself comparing him to Yenic. Yenic. She'd get up if only to spite him.

She inhaled deeply to send as much air to her lungs as she could. She braced her palms on the ground and tried to isolate her triceps so as not to disturb the still-tremoring muscles of her core. Then she focused on her biceps, telling them to heave her upward to her knees at least. She heard Gael's impressed grunt, but didn't feel his hands on her in aid. She hadn't expected it, in truth, but it would have made the shaky journey to her feet that much easier.

He said nothing when she gained her feet, merely lowered the bucket into the well and dipped a wooden cup in. This he offered to her.

She drank greedily, barely feeling the iciness of it against her teeth. In one swift wash, the sweat of pain and effort was gone. She offered him a grateful look.

Then promptly felt an icy rush flood back up her throat.

He looked at his boots in renewed disgust; Alaysha wasn't sure if she could keep the nervous laugh inside, so she dipped the cup into the bucket and emptied it repeatedly over his boots.

"That's enough for today," he said and strode back to Saxa's cottage. Alaysha had no choice but to follow.

And she was grateful beyond belief.

Each day for three days went like that: a quick meal with Yuri, who ignored her, a trip to the well. The only difference was Alaysha needed no one to help her from the bed or to walk. Gael said little. It was obvious he hated his new duty and it was equally obvious he felt the same about Alaysha.

She didn't mind. Rather, it felt familiarly comfortable to be hated again.

She made it to the well behind Gael in a huff of breathlessness and looked back towards the mountains that towered over Sarum. Yuri had built his city in a cleft of the mountain and bordered it on a wide river. He felt safe on at least two fronts but not all four. For a wise Emir, it was strange he chose to build beneath the mountain and not on top. It left him vulnerable from the most critical point. She wanted to ask Gael what he thought of this revelation, but he'd suddenly set his back to her and was shifting oddly side to side with his hand reaching backward, shepherding her behind him.

Curious. What could have the disdainful giant feeling so protective?

"What's the trouble?" she asked him only to be rewarded with a harsh shushing sound.

"Is it the other witch?"

"Yes," came the response, but he didn't sound convincing; in fact, he sounded rather stoic.

A scream of agony met Alaysha's ears and she immediately reached for a sword upon her back that was not there. She satisfied herself instead with a large rock someone had lain on the well's lip.

Gael pressed her against the well and she pushed back against him, furious that he would hinder her.

"Don't crowd me."

"I'll crowd you all I want."

"If I'm in danger, I don't need your protection."

He made to hold her by the shoulders. "The danger is not yours to meet, Witch."

She might be damaged and sore, but she could manoeuvre enough if she wanted. She feinted left, swallowing down a streak of burning pain, and then leaned right. By the time Gael recovered, she'd already seen what he was doing his best to hide from her.

Two swarthy men, very reminiscent of Drahl, were holding down a teenage girl inside the iron forger's cottage. In those brief seconds, it looked for all the world like they were pouring water over her throat.

Alaysha sent her power sniffing for water. The dankness of well came, sweat too. She tried to focus it, sent it to the smith's but all she got was a wash of wet heat so strong she felt as though her chin was on fire.

It was then she knew.

"They're scalding her."

She knew the smith; he was a hardworking man, captured during one of Yuri's first campaigns, so long ago she imagined the smith had forgotten he'd had a life before Sarum. Still, it made no sense he'd want to brand a chattel in such a way. It was too odd; most had their cheeks branded by iron, not this painful scalding.

She took the first painful steps towards the hovel. She didn't care how many men she had to face, or if she only carried a rock for defence, she would not see a young girl treated so inhumanely.

She felt a meaty hand on her shoulder.

"Stay," Gael told her.

"I will not." She pulled away and the weight of the stone made her balance, such as it was, awkward. She nearly fell. If he hadn't gripped her by the elbow, she would have.

"It's too late. It's done."

Alaysha listened and heard only the regular sounds of chickens and the snuffling of hounds. A roar of chatter met her ears from the good people of Sarum going about their chores, but no more shrieks. The girl had obviously fainted.

"She needs to be taken to the shaman."

He nodded. "Have no fear; she will be."

She looked at him, suspicious, but his expression kept the same stolid blankness. "How do you know this?"

She brought the image back to her mind. Teenage girl, black hair from what she could see. Most of Yuri's true tribe was fair; more evidence the girl was an outsider and probably a slave. Alaysha tried once more to get by Gael. He was as moveable as a castle wall.

"It's time you were back at Saxa's," he said and began steering her in the direction they'd come.

"I'm not weary." She rooted as best she could to her spot. "I want to walk more. I feel much stronger."

He didn't look as though he believed her. "Mmph," was all he said but he reached for her waist and Alaysha was certain he'd hoist her over his shoulder, except he paused as he pulled her close enough to do so. He paused, cocked his head, and pushed her instead to the ground.

An arrow landed just next to her ear as she fell with a thud. Even as she was wondering how he could possibly have heard it winging its way toward her, several more thunked into the earth around her. A girl screamed. A hound yelped and fell a few strides away, an arrow protruding from its belly. The chatter of Sarum's people doing daily chores turned instantly into chaos.

Rather than cover her head with her arms as instinct told her to do, Alaysha rolled toward the well and curved against it as best she could, opposite where the arrows seemed to be coming from. She'd wait till they'd spent and had to reload. She doubted the assailants had thought to rally the shots—there were just too many at once. By then, all unwounded citizens had found some shelter. A few lay on the ground moaning. Some wept. Alaysha steeled herself against their cries and sought out the source. And found it.

It seemed Gael had already done the same work. He had ducked and run toward the archer platform that defended the east wall, where at least a dozen archers were already pulling new notches from their quivers. So.

Those motley dressed men were not Yuri's after all. But whose?

Alaysha scanned the area. Besides the wounded worming their ways to cover, or people who'd succumbed to their shots, or dogs and chickens and the occasional pig who'd been shot, the only target was Gael. And he was flat out in the open—running, true, but flat open. He made a pleasantly easy target.

Before she could consider what she was doing, she pulled herself to her feet. She could draw some of the fire, but it wouldn't be enough. She knew they'd already set their sights on Gael. She'd have to remove him as a target just as they released, and by the look of it, that time was a few heartbeats away.

She breathed deeply and cupped her hand against her belly to offer it some support as she darted forward. His strides were long; she knew they were taking his measure even as he ran. She shouted at him, hoping to distract him for a second. Her side vision told her some of the archers had shifted their aim to her. It was now or never. She darted like a hare trying to outsmart a hound, still moving forward. He paused, taking the measure of the men he would be facing, their placements, their heights, and Alaysha could see the moment his gaze fell on the first of the men he'd have to kill. He'd never make it, but at least it gave Alaysha the time she needed to catch him. She launched herself forward and thudded into his chest.

He fell, pulling her down with him, and she used the force of it to roll, pulling him with her, yanking him atop her, then to their sides.

A dozen arrows struck the earth where they'd landed. She let go a pained grunt.

"Get up," he told her then was on his feet, using the short moments of reload to aim for the stairs.

Alaysha knew the archer's arrows were useless by now, that they would be pulling out whatever blades they'd secreted in their boots or breeches. She did as she was bid and got, staggering, to her feet.

Watching Gael would have been a thing of beauty but for the sight of blood and the hollow thunk of iron on bone as his sword leapt to service. He swept across the platform with seeming ease, swinging and connecting skulls, legs, arms, chests. When the quarters were too close for his sword to be of use, he twisted necks and pummelled with his fists and elbows.

When those at the back knew they'd lost and were losing their comrades, they scuttled for the other stairs.

She wasn't sure what she could do to help, in her condition and with no ready weapon to hand, but she stepped in front of the stairs anyway, thinking she could at least slow their escape.

The first of them launched a punch that was both awkward and poorly aimed. Luckily it also threw him off balance and she used his momentum to trip him over her leg and bring her elbow down on his neck. She had no hope against the flood of arms and chests that came after that. She did her best to avoid what blades she saw and concentrated on defense rather than attack, thinking that she only had to survive the remaining assailants and allow Gael to do his work. She knew at least three had gotten past her by the time she heard the sickening cracks of metal against skull more clearly.

Her eyes glazed at the men Gael was even now killing in front of her. He'd made his way nearly all the way through the archers. When she caught sight of his face, it was as bright as a newly forged blade. His eyes were almost mad in their delight; the short rash of beard he'd left unshaved, filled with dirt and blood, no longer looked blond but was the color of old rust. One cheekbone swelled beneath his glower. Bodies littered the stairs and on the platform; those who still lived had already made a hasty retreat past Alaysha.

All but one.

He was a young man, Alaysha could tell; his beard held the soft fuzz of new manhood. Gael towered over him, sword hanging, dripping at his side. His chest heaved with extended and expended effort. Alaysha thought Gael would kill the boy—she wasn't sure he could rise from the battle fog quickly enough to see how useful a captive would be. Someone had sent them, obviously. Yuri would want to know who.

Even as she was about to shout at him to spare the boy's life, an arrow bloomed in the youth's throat. His collapse against Gael made the warning unnecessary.

At sight of the shaft still quivering from the strike in the boy's neck, Gael's head swung toward her like a bull scoping out a new charge. His eyes rested on her, quickly running down her body, lingering on her stomach, and then darting to someplace behind her.

Someone was in back of her. A dozen strides away or more. She turned, giving a quick scan of the yard, ready to fight or flee.

And her eyes rested on Yenic.

CHAPTER 3

Alaysha thought she would collapse at sight of him, so great was the relief, the fury, and the outright pleasure that flooded her. Her first thought was to thank The Deities for his safe return. Her second was a much stronger impulse, one that wanted to demand that those same deities strike him down where he stood.

She knew Gael felt the same when he blustered by her.

"Don't," she said, knowing even as she did so that he was far past hearing.

Yenic's expression of victory died on his face as Gael squared off in front of him.

"You stupid boy. We could have questioned him." Gael clenched his fists at his sides and Alaysha could tell from the tightness of his back and shoulders that he was working at keeping calm. She shifted sideways, hoping to see Aedus behind Yenic somewhere, but realized that she felt a long trickle of wet running down her hip and that the effort of movement made her feel as though she had ice in her veins.

Her hands went immediately to her belly, fingers searching for the wound, hoping against every hope that she'd not torn the threadings. No such good fortune would be hers this day. While the raucous sounds of the two men arguing became more of a cloudy din in her ears, she had to fight the renewed blackness that wanted control over her sight. She'd done too much, of course. In the face of fire, however, any less would have meant death.

She didn't want to, but she had to let her legs go. It was that or pass out from the effort of standing. She opted to let her knees take her weight, and for her palms on the earth to keep her face from striking dirt. She could catch her breath if she let her head hang.

The sound of Yenic's startled shout wasn't enough to tear her gaze away from the ant that was industriously making its way home with what appeared to be a gob of flesh.

She felt hands on her shoulders. "Alaysha," she heard. "Alaysha. You're bleeding."

She peered up at Yenic's face. His eyes, still the color of honey, still sparking somewhere in the depths like a lazy fire. How she loved looking into those eyes.

"You're back," she said, but she didn't hear relief in her voice, only pain and anger. She felt sure he'd think it the pain of her wound.

He must have seen the shifting thoughts travel her face; his own took on an expression of confusion and hurt.

"What's wrong?" he asked.

Gael's scornful voice sounded over Alaysha's back saving her from blurting out that she was hurt, that he hurt her.

"What's wrong?" Gael bellowed. "She's hurt, you fool."

It wasn't what Yenic meant and Alaysha knew it. She also knew Gael wouldn't understand. She saw him twist to look past Alaysha's shoulder into what was a very red, very condescending face.

She tried to push herself to her haunches with the aim of standing.

"Let me help," Yenic said. His palm on her back felt hot, too hot for mere body temperature but then he was always so, she remembered.

Dirt got scuffed into her eye and she yelped. Gael's boots, toeing Yenic to the ground and shuffling closer to Alaysha. She felt herself being lifted, those meaty hands beneath her knees and shoulders, her body pressed against his. She caught him looking down at her even as he spoke to Yenic.

"You go to Yuri. Tell him you killed his only means of finding out who ordered this attack. I'll see to the witch." His tone sounded harsh, even to Alaysha's ears but she'd rarely felt safer. She wished it could be Yenic who held her, but she knew he belonged to his mother—the witch she had yet to meet, who knew the secrets of controlling the power. She tried to stifle any sense of relief she felt when Yenic started to argue, but then it didn't matter because Gael was striding effortlessly away from the curtain and past the well. He smelled of sweat and blood and she could feel his heart beating against her ribcage with such mad frenzy she understood just how natural his ability for war was. How much his body needed it.

The only thing that moved as frantically was her own stomach, twisting on itself.

"I don't feel so well," she admitted.

He made an odd sound. "You've torn the threads. Saxa had thought you well healed. You must not be good stock. Good stock heals better than that."

"I tore them saving you."

"You tore them getting in my way."

She was incensed. "If I hadn't knocked you down, you'd have been shot." She glared at him, but all she could see were his nostrils. Both flared angrily.

"You threw yourself at me. I had to roll over so you wouldn't get shot."

"I remember it differently."

"Remember it as you will."

She could feel herself slipping. "You're dropping me," she said, but barely heard her own complaint; she thought the clouds must have drifted over the sun, blocking out the light, then a tiny piercing glare crept back into her vision. Gael was looking down at her.

"I won't drop you no matter how slippery you get."

It was such an odd thing to say, she couldn't help trying a weak smile.

"Don't leave, Witch. Stay with me."

She had nowhere to go, did she? But the way he called her witch this time sounded different, almost worried. She had to work to keep her eyes open now that the pain was coming back. Strange, she hadn't felt it during battle, but then she'd heard plenty of stories of warriors hacking mercilessly at the enemy even as their own bellies were torn open. The battle beast, some called it, the drive within to survive even as death was creeping upon your limbs, to take life as though it could return yours to you. She realized then why Gael's tone had sounded so worried. And why Yenic, Deities take him for his lies, had looked so concerned.

"Am I dying?" she asked, afraid, and at the same time hopeful, that Yenic's concern might really have meant her father had been wrong about his intent, that he really did care about her.

"No, dear girl."

Dear girl? Saxa's voice. Must be. And indeed, it was feminine, she realized as the voice came again. She must have passed out.

"Just suffering the wound spirit. Your body is complaining about its injury."

She felt herself being lowered again onto the bed and realized as Gael eased away that his tunic was bright red where she'd rested against it. So he was right. She wasn't a good healer. She felt such shame she wanted everyone to go away and leave her be.

"Get the shaman, Gael." Saxa pulled at Alaysha's feet and raised them onto a bunch of furs and pillows. "Stay with me, Alaysha. Are you cold?"

Alaysha could barely nod, but Saxa caught it and threw the fur over her. It didn't matter. It held no warmth and the shivering threatened to make her teeth click together.

All that healing, all that work, all that killing and fighting, and for it to come to this: such pain and nausea and cold from a few torn stitches. Deities, the cold. She couldn't stop shivering to save her soul. What if this time death stole her? She wouldn't see Aedus again. Or Barruch. She'd never know who her people truly were or why her father had wanted them all dead. Worse still, she'd not get to feel Yenic's hand on hers again, hear his voice in her ear, his lips on hers…

Fear crept in before she could think of anything else but dying, and just as quickly, she could taste the salt in Saxa's tears.

The power had come again and this time, she wasn't sure she could stop it.

Chapter 4

It was the tears that reminded her. She knew the water she tasted was from Saxa's tears, barely shed before they were psyched from her. Sweet deities, not Saxa. Alaysha thought of her dream and focused as quickly as she could on the one's her nohma had collected those years ago. "There's magic in tears," Saxa had said, and nohma had certainly believed it true. Why else would she have used them to bond her to Yenic?

That was the memory she'd struggled to remember since she'd awoken. Tears. It was no coincidence, not in this moment, to remember it. And whether it was the unknown deities she'd heard her nohma pray to all those years that gave her back the memory, or her nohma herself, didn't matter.

She let herself taste them, yes, but she worked very hard to send the fluid back from where it came. Saxa wept from fear. Alaysha psyched from fear. There had to be balance there somewhere. Yenic had told her it was about balance. If he could be believed, then to combat the power of hatred, you used the power of love. To psych fluid from the living, you had to want death.

From clouded eyes, she watched a mist collect and hover in the room. It seemed to take long moments, but Alaysha knew from experience that she was going under like a woman sinking into a bath of warmth, that the power was tricking her in terms of time. She knew that within three or five breaths it would be over.

She didn't need the water. She didn't want it. What she wanted was for Saxa to live. For the water to come from elsewhere if it must, to return to the poor woman even as it seeped away.

Surely there must be some way to stop it.

Gael burst into view and was pulling Saxa away just as the mist let go its burden and sent a spray of water in droplets all over the chamber. His curses were enough to make Alaysha cringe where she lay and she came back to herself so quickly she could have been assaulted with cold water.

"What good is a witch who can't control her own power?" He bellowed, and Alaysha couldn't disagree.

She felt someone's hand on her: the shaman's, it seemed, fleeting over her belly, probing the threadings.

"Not as bad as we thought," he murmured. "More the insult to a healing psyche brought on the spell, than the wound. See? It's already clotting. Quite nicely too." He was mumbling to himself it seemed, because he spoke back as though he was the second man listening. "We do thread well. And the balsam has done the trick. Oh, yes. But why so much blood for such a small reopening? Oh. We see a second wound. Superficial only. Yes. It begs more threading."

His finger poked into a newly sore area and took Alaysha by surprise. She let go a shriek that made her wish she had been able to keep her mouth clamped shut.

The result was a pinch on the cheek equally as painful and she thought he was doing it deliberately, but dared not complain.

"We don't see why the Emir keeps her and not the other," he said. "Far too much bother, this one."

"I can hear you."

"She thinks it matters to us if she can hear. She does. She believes we shame ourselves, but a shaman such as Theron feels no shame. Why should we?"

"Because a witch has power." She managed between gritted teeth. It seemed now she was warm, she was too warm.

"Such power. Yes. She needs a shaman twice in ten turns. It's a good thing this Theron has no such power."

She heard something strange in his voice, as though he was forcing himself to speak and didn't like it one bit. His callous manner made Alaysha want to strike at him, but she knew he was working to make her whole. That alone was worth allowing him to keep some dignity. When he began threading something sharp and painful into her side, she quickly rethought her decision.

He chuckled aloud when she sucked in a breath to brace against the stitching. She caught his eye as he pulled through the last of the threads, and she thought she detected concern then decided she'd not seen enough concern in her lifetime to recognize it.

"Is Saxon all right?" she asked. She had a sudden moment of panic that the baby hadn't lived through the episode. He very nearly hadn't made it through the last one.

The shaman let his gaze lower to her belly, then covered her over carefully with the linen tunic Saxa had helped her into just days before. It was a gift to replace the heavy leather one that had gotten ruined during Drahl's attack, but now this one, too, was all bloody.

"I asked—"

"We heard." He looked directly at her. "Saxon has not yet returned from the nursery. The witch harmed only the one who cared for her in the first place."

"Harmed?" Her voice was so shrill, she barely recognized it.

The shaman pushed himself to his feet and cast an inquiring look about the cottage.

"Looks contained, though, does it not? Yes. Yes. It does, however it's very, very wet." He scowled down at her. "Would that the witch had the power to clean her mess. Now. It's off to see the good wife. And the Emir. He will want to know of it. Know of it? No doubt he knows already and would come to strike the witch down; and this Theron with her if we didn't beat a hasty retreat from this nest of ill-used power."

She wanted to protest but hadn't the heart. It was truth, all of it. Even the words he answered to himself. She decided to let him go while she waited for Yuri. If he wasn't angry enough to see her killed, finally, he'd at least want to chastise her into full guilt and shame—and no doubt find a way to use that to his benefit.

She knew the old wound was again sealed and balsamed—it stank and stuck to the wrappings so she could feel it when she moved, and the new wound had been merely stitched back together and given a few threads. Superficial, he'd said—that meant she didn't need to worry about it pulling apart and bleeding her out. She must have gotten it from one of the archer's blades during their full-on escape.

Just standing, even supporting herself by holding onto the table, made her feel more able to withstand what she knew was coming.

Yuri was moments behind Theron, and Alaysha was grateful she'd thought enough to work herself to her feet. Gael was behind him and for some reason his face was far redder than Yuri's. His eyes far angrier. But he said nothing, merely stood behind Yuri as though to protect his back from anyone thoughtlessly, or intentionally entering.

She wasn't prepared for Yuri's reaction at all.

"It's good Gael thought to bring you here," he said, and Gael shuffled his feet, doing his best to avoid

Alaysha's eye. And while she was unprepared for Yuri's reaction, she was flat-out shocked at her own.

"You care that little for the woman who bore your heir?" She felt the quake taking her legs and had to shift in place to make them believe she was moving of her own accord, consciously making the choice. "You are relieved I put her in danger?" She looked him squarely in the eyes and asked the question that threatened to buckle her knees altogether.

"Is she dead?"

When he didn't answer Alaysha sought Gael's face. He'd not be able to keep that from his eyes, no matter how stoic his expression.

"Is she dead?" she asked him. The reward of a nearly imperceptible shake of his head nearly stole her strength anyway.

It seemed that despite answering, Gael would wait for Yuri to speak. No one said anything for a time and Alaysha wanted nothing more than to collapse again onto the bed. So much for being a trained warrior—nearly felled twice by a mere bit of steel.

Yuri finally bid her sit and took a chair himself. He faced off against her across the table.

"Saxa is fine. But she has lost much fluid, so I have a woman feeding her water and honey until the shaman reaches her."

"You had the shaman come to me first?" It was almost too much to stand.

"Theron was nearly here anyway when your Yenic—"

"He's not my Yenic."

Yuri took a moment to give her a lazy smile of satisfaction, then pressed on.

"When Yenic came to me with news of the attack, I knew Gael would keep you safe."

"And Saxa in danger."

"She's not in danger. She is a casualty like many others. She has courage, that one." His voice was filled with pride.

Alaysha was ashamed. She couldn't stand remembering the paths her power had taken trying to steal into Saxa's pores. She did her best to block them from coming to mind. "I know."

"You think I could have kept her away from you?"

Alaysha couldn't answer that, but tried. "Still. The shaman should have gone to your wife first. She bore your child. You love her." She nearly choked on the clump in her throat.

Yuri held his hand up. "She is worthy of being so only because she knows her worth. And yours. And the value of keeping the city intact."

Gael's cough made Alaysha want to hurl something at him. She worked hard to keep her warrior's calm.

"The truth is," Yuri said, "Saxa is even now telling the shaman what she needs and doubtless Theron is trying to ignore her."

"You can't know that."

His white brows lifted delicately. "I can't? I know her better than you do." He turned to Gael for confirmation.

"She'll be giving him orders," Gael said.

"Then why send for the shaman at all?" It was off point, and a useless question in the argument of who should be sent Theron first, but Alaysha didn't care. She was beginning to feel contrary.

Yuri grinned. "The truth. Again it must rear its head, eh, Gael?"

Gael chuckled and shifted his booted feet against the floor. "Saxa is a terrible seamstress."

It wasn't an expected answer, and it was so far afield of what she believed of Saxa, that Alaysha couldn't help smiling. That explained the young wife's constant worry over breaking the threads despite the increasingly healing wound. She was afraid she'd have to stitch them again.

"Is she truly alive?" she asked and only let go a breath when Yuri nodded.

"Gael brought her straight to me. We might have to find a wet nurse for Saxon for a few days, but she will live."

Alaysha relaxed, but Yuri wasn't done.

"How did you do it?" he asked.

Confused, she looked up at him. "Do what?"

"Harness the power?"

Even Gael looked interested in the answer.

Ah, the reason he was here, finally. "I don't know."

His narrow-gazed scrutiny indicated he didn't believe her, but he nodded anyway.

"You will continue to walk daily with Gael," he said. "Until you are strong enough to begin the work of healing."

"When will I see the fire witch?" She couldn't help hoping she would finally meet the woman who could make Saxa nervous and who could hold Yenic in her power and who could, if the rumors were true, control the very flame itself. He ignored the question and set a path for the door and she knew she had to content herself to wait for the answer, knowing it would come in its time whether she wanted it now or not. She wasn't content, however, to wait for the next answer, and she threw the question at him before he could yank the door open.

"Where's Yenic?" she demanded.

Without turning to face her, he answered, and she could hear the smile in his tone. The satisfaction.

"I'm having him flogged."

CHAPTER 5

Gael was left standing where Yuri had left, and Alaysha worked her way over to him. She knew her face was a mask of outrage, and at the same time she tried hard to tell herself she should be feeling nothing for the man who had let her believe he was her Arm; that they were the only two left from her tribe, that there were others like her. So many secrets he'd kept, he had no right to her concern.

"Does he speak truth?" She knew by the feeling in the pit of her stomach even as she asked the question that her father wasn't lying.

"Have you known him to speak otherwise?"

Alaysha thought for a moment, remembering her discussion with Yuri just after his lead scout had tried to kill her and she'd ended up here. Yuri had told her he'd never lied to her, and despite some very harsh things, he had always said them. She tried to imagine Yenic's smooth skin stretched before the lash, laid open, and knew she couldn't keep a warrior's calm in the knowledge of that.

"Take me to him."

"You don't command me."

She moved even closer toward Gael, and while she expected him to back away, he stood stoic. She caught an odd but fleeting expression on his face, as though he feared her, then it was gone.

"I won't hurt you," she said.

A slow smile spread across his lips, but he didn't respond. She marvelled at how much that smile could change his face, even when it was fleeting. His eyes changed from that smokey grey they appeared to be to that stunning green and blue she knew they were.

She tried again, this time meekly. "It's a request, Gael. Not a command."

He watched her thoughtfully. She wasn't sure what flitted through his mind, but it was plenty; she could at least see that.

"Please. Every breath of delay means one less to stop this atrocity."

"Come, then," he told her and without elaborating, was out the door. He didn't bother to check that she followed or if she struggled to do so. She made the decision to push down the discomfort she felt in her side and press on, no matter how winded or weak she grew. She was Yuri's daughter when it came down to it, and at least the one thing she could claim was a stoic ability to do her duty.

He led her through the courtyard past the well. The good people of Sarum had already begun filtering back to complete their daily chores, as if the attack was nothing more than a faded memory. The bodies had already been removed but for those of a couple of chickens and dogs. Several feral cats were picking at the carcasses and squabbling loudly.

Alaysha had expected Yenic to be strapped to the pillory in the midst of the square as most criminals were so that any passers-by could watch and be warned. She'd seen a man flogged before when she was in her fifteenth season and the man hadn't survived it. What had survived though were the charges the caller had shouted to the crowd each time his lash split the air: that insolence to the Great Yuri would not be tolerated. She'd found out later that man was Saxa's father and the insolence was to lay cruel hands on a woman Yuri had recently noticed and come to want. Doubtless the man had no knowledge of Yuri's desire when he'd beaten his daughter in public, and more likely even than that, it was probably that latest beating that drew Yuri's attention in the first place.

Strange. She hadn't thought of that in a long time. She'd long ago learned to bury unpleasant memories; the power came within such an incredible memory that it was often as much a curse as the power. They came hand-in-hand, it seemed, the better to remember the paths of each drop of fluid. But it meant she stored a vast archive of unpleasantness, and to survive — to harden herself, as Yuri had taught her — was to place a good bit of soil over each thing that could cause her pain.

The question was: why had that flogging caused her enough pain to bury the memory in the first place?

"Do you remember the last flogging in Sarum, Gael?"

From behind him she saw his back stiffen, but he forged ahead of her without pause. She took advantage of his seeming vulnerability. Oh, her father would be proud, using a painful thing to control another person.

"We will have to stop it," she told him.

"Yuri commands me," he said from over his shoulder.

"Yuri is angry. He's not thinking clearly. You can't do this to Yenic."

"Yuri always thinks clearly."

That was true, and Alaysha knew it. The other, nestled truth was that Yuri was not flogging Yenic in public. Insolence was a crime that could be used as a teaching tool. So why was this happening away from the courtyard?

Logic told her it was about more than disobedience and anger.

"He can't flog him where Yenic's mother will discover it, can he?"

Rather than answer, Gael turned in the direction of the Keep and led her toward the back curtain. The river was beyond that, and a few strides east was the mountain Yuri had hewn a small castle into.

The sick liquidity of memory started to move within her the closer she got. She followed Gael through an iron door set into the rock face's natural opening and then into the dank, dripping maw of what Yuri called the witch's home.

It had been home, once. Just after Nohma died and Alaysha had gone mad with grief. She knew how far in they would have to travel, how many steps it would take to get to the bathhouse. How many drips of water would fall in an inhale, and beyond that, how many drops would fall in a turn, in a week, a fortnight. A season.

She shuddered, but refused to let the memory take her. She was here for Yenic. He might have used her, he might yet have to prove he wasn't trying to manipulate her, but he didn't deserve pain. Not this pain, anyway.

"You need come no farther with me," she told Gael. She knew where Yenic would be.

Gael halted and turned. There was still enough light from the outside that she could see his face and the torch on the wall sconce played with the shadows that kept trying to alter his features. She tried to read the strange expression she saw there.

She interpreted it how she wanted even if he wasn't concerned for her. "I'll be fine." She stepped closer and without thinking, reached for his forearm. She felt him nearly snatch it away, but he did allow the touch.

"You don't fear me," she said.

He stared into her eyes. "I fear nothing."

She gave him a questioning look.

"It's not fear?" She echoed.

"Fear is for those who don't know their own power."

He was talking about her, whether he knew it or not, he was talking about her and maybe she was reading more into it all than was there.

"Those who know their own power," he went on, "know its limits and prepare for them."

"What are your limits, Gael?" She looked over the hair that shone even here in the shadows, the broad jaw and the way he towered over her, over nearly everything so that he was forever looking down at things. She looked him over and thought his limits must have something to do with feeling above it all.

"My limit is that I know no fear." He pulled away from her at last, but let his forearm linger just beneath her touch. "Go to your boy," he said. "See if you can change what is about to happen to him."

Alaysha watched him go back towards the entrance and stop just close enough to the door that he couldn't be seen from the outside unless someone was looking directly in. He put his back against the cave wall and slid down to his haunches. He could have been an innocuous boulder near the entrance, but Alaysha knew that if anyone came in, he would not let them pass.

She took a deep breath and moved deeper into the cave, veered right automatically, where outside light couldn't get in, and headed forward, lit only by the torches and beeswax candles in the crevices made of natural rock. A steady sweat of water ran down the stone, and into gunnels carved into the floor after centuries of movement. She knew she was climbing a slight slope because her wind came up, reminding her that she wasn't quite fully healed. Her wind had risen those years ago, too, but only because she'd already used up most of her air with the grief of tears.

Before she could stop it, the memory was upon her. She could hear Yuri's voice again, too, if she tried, telling her to stop her whimpering. To steel herself like any great warrior would. How could a soldier kill if he cried like a baby over a simple death.

She'd had the audacity to argue—she was a girl, not a boy, and the simple death she had dealt was her nohma's. Had he no heart?

He'd struck her, of course. A quick backhand across the cheek, and she refused to rub the pain out, instead facing him with tears running down her cheeks the same way they ran down the walls of stone. Then, though, as they didn't now, the fluid from the walls rose to a mist and clouded the cavern. It rained too. Hard, aggressive, and piercing rain that seemed to move straight from the gunnels, to the cloud, to Yuri's face, and to the ground again.

"You can keep at me all day, Witch," he'd told her. "There's enough water in this mountain that you'll never psych it dry." Then he pulled her mercilessly into what he called the bathhouse.

It was a cavernous enclave with holes in the earth so wide a man could bath in them. Some bubbled and frothed like wash water saturated with soap. Some lay stagnant but hot, sending wafts of steam to the ceiling. Now, as then, Yuri stood in the center of it all with his arms crossed, feet planted authoritatively.

She wasn't surprised to see him step from memory to reality. Nor was she surprised to see the wooden table heaving with instruments of all kinds, the setup of shackles and wood that stretched Yenic's broad back out into one full length of arm. Fingertip to fingertip, the shackles pulled at his wrist and the manacles, with their Yuri-created finger holds, pulled each muscle all the way from neck to middle finger as taut as possible. Yenic didn't even need the strength of his legs to stand so. The shackles kept him erect.

Next to Yuri stood the Carrion, as Alaysha called him. She'd probably been told his name once, but didn't care to remember it. He held a long leather whip in one hand and cradled the length of it in the other. She knew she had arrived in time, but she also knew she didn't have much to spare.

"Please, don't," she said, and while her father didn't so much as move, the Carrion bobbed his head in her direction and gave her a lazy grin.

"Too many memories, Witch?" he asked her.

She'd never been flogged by the Carrion; the only man who had been, she realized just then, was Saxa's father, but she'd certainly been beaten by the Carrion. Most times she told herself Yuri hadn't known about the punches to the stomach, and in truth, it might have been true. He never hit her where bruises could be seen — only in the ribs, the shins, buttocks. He beat the whimpering nearly out of her without worry of dying a witch-contrived death. Not that she hadn't tried, but because her power psyched always the most readily available fluid before it pulled at the liquid from a man. And the cavern had such an abundance of water it couldn't create a cloud large enough to hold the water before it came down again.

In the days when her power was unpredictable, but weaker, she couldn't steal his fluid no matter how much she tried.

Things could be different now.

"I don't fear my memories," she told him and heard her father chuckle.

"She's trained now Corrin," he told the man. "Far more powerful than she was when you first taught her."

"Is that what he called it?" she asked. "Training?"

Yuri looked Corrin over and new suspicion crept across his features so subtly and so quickly, Alaysha doubted Corrin saw it. She thought it time he discovered the truth of her childhood mysteries. Anything to keep the lash from Yenic's back.

"What exactly was he to be teaching me, Father?"

Yuri swung his gaze back to her. His face was controlled and complacent, but his eyes were sharp and bright even in the torch and candlelight.

"He was to teach you what you learned—control over your weeping and sentimentality."

"But not of her power."

Yenic's voice. So he was aware and listening. Thank the Deities.

"You would do well to stay silent," Yuri told him and Alaysha watched the subtle movements of Yenic's shoulders and wondered whether he was laughing or trying to take a breath. She moved toward him and spoke just loudly enough for him to hear.

"How long?"

"A few moments, no more."

She breathed relief. At least he hadn't stood like that for too long. She'd managed it herself for only long enough to receive a few staunch blows before losing her leg strength and having to hang there by her wrists. That didn't stop the beatings, though, no matter how much her wrists hurt.

"You thought to flog him father, and then what? Have him return to his mother? What would happen then?"

Yuri shrugged his indifference. "Perhaps you should tell me why a man would kill the last person who could explain an attack on his people and then not be disciplined."

The Carrion mumbled his agreement and Alaysha glared at him. "Careful, beast," she said. "Or I might enlighten Yuri of your training methods."

Again, Yuri looked at Corrin, but this time there was no change in expression, even subtly. It was pure examination, that look. Taking in each inch of Corrin and assessing, processing, storing what he saw. That was enough to satisfy her. She turned again to Yenic and reached for his rib cage where she knew the tattaus were. She touched his skin and felt it pimple under her fingers even though the flesh was still hot to her touch. "I know. You're cold in here," she said and Yenic grunted.

"Never cold," he murmured.

The way his voice sounded: intimate, warm, she had to remind herself he couldn't be trusted. Not yet. No matter how badly she wanted to be able to forgive him, she had to remind herself she just didn't want him to be flogged. No more. She turned to Yuri, leaving her hand on Yenic, thinking the connection could lend him some strength.

"You know it would be foolish to harm him," she told Yuri.

"His mother doesn't even know he's returned."

"And so when she does she will find him abused, or is it that you plan to keep him here until he's healed? Because that would be foolish. He'll grow only weaker."

Yuri shrugged. "Then he should tell me why he killed that boy."

She could feel Yenic trying to twist around as he spoke and she reached for one of the manacles. It had a special catch that if pressed, would snap open.

"I told you," Yenic said. "I didn't know he was the last one." His arm hung loose by his side, but it enabled him to swing to face them as he spoke.

Yuri stepped closer. "Who were they?" It was clear by his tone that he believed Yenic knew.

Yenic shook his head. "We saw them about a day ago and crept up to them. Listened to them."

"We." Yuri didn't move but it almost seemed as though his voice had taken several steps forward. "Meaning you and the girl."

"Aedus," Alaysha guessed. "Drahl's slave girl."

Yuri nodded, inpatient. "Where is she?"

"She stayed behind in the forest by the river."

That information bothered Alaysha until she remembered how tenacious the twelve season's girl could be. Surely, she'd be fine near the river, where she could drink if thirsty and forage for eggs or berries. That still didn't answer why she hadn't come into the city with him, and Alaysha wanted to know more than Yuri did.

"Why did she stay behind?"

Yenic's yellow-eyed gaze turned on Alaysha. "You told me to keep her safe."

Yes, she had. Back when she thought he was her Arm and not his mother's, when she thought she was the only remaining witch with powers of her type, the only surviving member of her tribe. She believed he would keep the girl safe for her. She believed so much then.

"Safest to leave her alone?"

"Safer then here, I suppose." He might not have been able to shrug, but his voice implied it. It made Alaysha think about how safe the girl actually had been in the city, driven to forage as she fled her master, the infamous Drahl, who mistreated everything he owned—people included.

Yuri seemed he'd had enough. "It matters not. The girl is where the girl is. The real question is who were they? Who attacked my people?"

Yenic swung his gaze toward Yuri, whose feet were planted apart, his arms still crossed. In the dim light he looked tired but determined. "I told you. I don't know."

"I heard the words." Yuri turned finally and studied Corrin. "Take him out of the shackles."

Corrin scowled miserably but did as he was told. When Yenic's arm let go, it was accompanied by a low groan from its owner. Alaysha had a flash of memory deep in her own cells that reminded her how painful and how pleasurable that release was. She noticed Corrin's slow grin of satisfaction and wanted to see him dead right then.

"Come, then," Yuri said and started out of the bathhouse in purposeful strides that gave Alaysha a short moment of panic that she would be left alone inside again. It wasn't until she felt Yenic take her left side and she could smell the sweat on him from the insult to his body that she felt as though she could move. She wanted to reach out to him and might have if Corrin hadn't pushed them both aside to catch up to Yuri.

Yuri stopped abruptly, just where the bathhouse met the tunnel that snaked out towards the entrance. Corrin stood next to him, waiting, until Yuri looked over his shoulder at Alaysha.

"Put him in the chains."

"Him? Corrin?"

Yuri's brow lifted. "Corrin? I thought you called him the Carrion?"

Alaysha would keep his gaze. She would. She would not look down in the face of that bald knowledge.

Corrin backed up before Alaysha could protest or agree. "You've lost your mind," he told Yuri.

"I have lost one thing only, and it is not my mind." Yuri stepped closer to Corrin whose face shifted from disbelief to panic. Strange how a man so adept at offering pain could quake so. Yuri seemed oblivious to the man's fear, and Alaysha could see how his own training was used to great effect. He took in Alaysha's rigid posture, her dreams realized, true, but a fearful thing to see occur nonetheless, and he advanced on Corrin once more.

"If you do not retreat to those shackles, I will kill you right now."

A sickening kind of hope crept across Corrin's face. He knew he would not die in this moment. Alaysha could have felt sorry for him until Yenic took her hand. It was hot, too hot, and clammy with sweat. She didn't have to look to the table next to those shackles to be reminded of the tools that lay there waiting for use, to know how afraid he'd been. How badly the Carrion wanted to use them.

She lost her pity.

"Will you choose, Corrin, or must I?" Yuri asked.

Corrin shuffled back into the cavern and stood waiting beneath the shackles.

Yuri nodded at Alaysha. "Bind him."

Wordless, she did as he told her. Corrin glared into her face, and although she wouldn't take in his eyes, she knew they were filled with hate.

"I was too easy on you," he whispered.

"My father would have killed you otherwise."

He chuckled low. "Your father pretends he doesn't know how I trained you. Are you truly that stupid?"

She said nothing, merely jerked his wrists into the manacles, stretched them, pinched his fingers with the clamps.

"Truth is," he said. "I told him everything. How you wept. How your ribs sounded when they cracked. How much you enjoyed our time together."

She gathered spit. How dare he? How dare he make her remember. She grabbed his chin with her fingers to hold him fast, looked into his black eyes, and sent the gob straight at him.

"You can rot in here," she said.

He acted as though the fluid wasn't there. "I would if he didn't need me so badly." He chuckled. "You go with your boy. I'll just wait until Yuri returns for me."

Her legs were trembling, but she managed to leave him and travel out of the bathhouse and into the intermittent dark of the tunnel. Yenic took the back, her father the front. She was so engrossed in her thoughts she wasn't aware Yuri had stopped until she walked into his back.

He turned and looked down at her. The blue eyes that rarely met hers and that could be so striking were merciless in their directness, with the flickering light of torches playing over them.

"You told me, before, the thing that made you agree to kill me was because I never gave you a choice about killing others."

She said nothing; she had said it, just nine or so turns ago, when he wanted to know why she was willing to put him and the entire city to her power to save just one girl: Aedus.

He looked over her shoulder in the direction of the snaking tunnel. "You have that choice now."

Kill Corrin? Surely he didn't mean it. She pulled her arms across her chest. So many times beneath the Carrion's hand had she wished it. Dreamed it when she passed out, begged for it when she'd psyched as much moisture as she could from the cavern and still there was too much to pull from him.

She felt Yuri's hand on her shoulder. "He will stay there until you decide." He snuffed with finality and turned from her. In seconds he was out of sight, lost in the darkness before she felt Yenic behind her again.

"Let's get out of here."

She couldn't speak to him either; she was so filled with conflicting thoughts and emotions. Not knowing whom to trust: her father who'd always used her or this boy who had pretended to love her and had lied to her. Knowing she was now being given permission to kill again, but only by her choice, when she'd always just been ordered to do so. Ordered, but never wanting to take life. The flood of thoughts were enough to get her feet moving by way of escape from them.

She was just seeing the far-off light of the iron bars when she realized Gael was still there, a hunched form next to the stone he'd settled against.

Yuri must have passed right by him and Gael, obviously feeling guilty about having led Alaysha into the mountain face, had opted to stay hunched next to the wall.

"Gael?" she said, testing her voice.

No response nor movement came from the pile of leather and boots.

"Gael?" She said again, and Yenic brushed past her to put his hands on the man's shoulders.

"Oh no," he murmured.

No? Oh no? That couldn't be good. "Yenic? What's wrong?"

He stood from his squat at Gael's side and pointed down at the man's throat. It took a few moments, a few steps, and a close examination to see a tiny quill jutting from just behind Gael's ear.

"What is it?" She didn't truly want to know the answer.

Yenic folded his arms across his chest, exasperated. "Aedus," he said.

CHAPTER 6`

It took the two of them to stretch Gael out into the sunshine beyond the doors. By the time they had dragged him through the iron gates and laid him flat, Alaysha was both out of breath and weak. It had taken all of her command of herself to work without giving in to the still lingering pain of her injury.

Yenic pulled the quill and passed it to Alaysha who inspected it. Porcupine. Hollow and empty. She shrugged at Yenic. "I don't understand." She leaned over and listened at Gael's mouth again. Yes. Breath. Shallow, as though he was sleeping but not quite under enough. "He's alive."

"Of course he is. Do you think Aedus a murderer?"

An old woman with a basket of onions strolled by and, seeing the witch and a man staring down at what was obviously one of Yuri's soldiers, gave them an abrupt wide berth.

"We should get him out of sight," Yenic said. "We don't want to make people nervous."

"How long will he be out?"

Yenic pursed his lips, thinking. "The last batch had me out for a couple of hours."

"A couple of hours? You?" Alaysha stared at him. "Last batch?"

He shrugged one shoulder deferentially. "She found a new pastime while we were searching for Edulph."

It sounded like there was much more background, but it also didn't seem the time to talk about it. Instead, Alaysha gave her attention to Gael. "So, if he's out for a couple of hours, we need to get him out of sight."

Yenic said nothing but gave her an I-told-you-so look.

"Yes," she answered. "That's what you said, I know." She scanned the area of the curtain, searching for a good spot to put him, and finding none, stated the obvious. "Why don't we just bring him to his sister? It's not as though we've done anything wrong."

Simple enough, except she was already aching from the exertion of dragging him into the sunlight. She hoped Yenic would come up with a better plan.

Yenic reached for Gael's feet. "If you say so, but you take the head part. I don't want to be anywhere near that mouth if he wakes up." He lifted. Grunted. Alaysha reached beneath Gael's shoulders and when she tried to heft him, found she couldn't keep from wincing and letting go. He fell with a thunk to the ground.

"I can't," she said.

Yenic chewed his lip thoughtfully. "Hurts too much?"

"I kind of overdid it during the attack."

"Kind of?"

She sighed, looking down at Gael's head and settled for easing onto the dirt and pulling his head onto her lap. "I guess I got stabbed a little bit."

Yenic dropped the feet and managed to look annoyed and concerned at the same time. "Stabbed."

Said baldly like that, it did sound a little extreme.

She nodded. Gael's head fit nicely into the crook of her thighs and she truly did feel winded and sore.

"You go get his sister. She'll know what to do with him. I'll stay here."

A hound snuffled up to her as she sat. It had a white spot on the top of its nose that reminded her of Barruch. She would go to the stables later and bring him a parsnip from Saxa's kitchen. That was providing she wasn't angry at her for getting Gael into this condition. Yenic had yet to leave and she wondered what the hesitation was.

"What are you waiting for?"

"I don't know," he said. "Something just doesn't feel right."

"Because it isn't. Aedus is inside somewhere shooting people with sleeping potions, Corrin is in the bathhouse waiting to have his fate decided, I'm sore as a cat with a cut tail, and Gael is lying here on the ground with his head in the lap of a woman he hates. What could be right?"

Yenic chewed the inside of his cheek thoughtfully, but finally sighed and gave in. She watched him leave, thinking how peculiar he would look to the citizens of Sarum with his chest bare, tattaus running up one side and beneath his arm. He stood out in other ways too. Most of Sarum was fair—as Yuri's original tribe was fair and large, but Yenic's fairness was different. He was wiry strong, not broad like Yuri's people. Her people. Well, half her people. And he was much shorter.

Still. That wasn't all of it. The people of Sarum, original and captured and enslaved, had all adopted an air. They seemed to know subconsciously that they were from within and went about their business as though no danger could touch them. In a word, they were oblivious.

The soldiers were somewhat different. They were wary, but they too expected the city to keep them safe from those without. Yenic, however, stepped lightly, bounded where he could, as though in one movement he could avoid sudden danger. He never took a straight route. She watched him seeming to meander through the throngs and clusters of people, but was decidedly intent on his direction. He never swung his arms. He had an economy of movement that spoke of a warrior's training, but he had something else that the Sarum warriors did not. Something she couldn't name.

She thought back to the time beneath the early morning sun, back at the oasis, when Aedus had gone off and they'd thought she was just foraging. She could easily remember the feel of his hands on her skin, the taste of his mouth with its lingering sweetness of honey and peaches, how filled with need she was to have him closer, even though they were already pressed hard against each other.

She felt as though someone was watching her.

"What are you doing?"

She looked down into Gael's face. Yes. Someone was. She thought her face must be burning red.

"Sleep well?" She asked him and tried not to compare the eyes she saw beneath hers to the honeyed eyes that had looked into her own just moments before. Tried and failed. She wasn't sure whose were more captivating. She told herself it didn't matter.

Gael groaned and rolled onto his side. "I wasn't sleeping."

"Of course not. I snore when I'm awake too."

He glared at her and tried to get up, grabbed his head and weaved back and forth.

"Careful," she said. "You've not been awake long."

He didn't open his eyes, but his tone told her if he did, his nasty glare would not have left. "I told you, I was not asleep. I don't sleep."

"Ever."

"When I need it, yes. But not on duty."

"You must have needed it, then," she said and thought she shouldn't have pushed him so. He obviously had no idea about Aedus.

He struggled to his feet and towered over her, looking down. She thought he would reach out to help her up, but then he took a deliberate step backward.

"I don't feel right," he said. "What did you do to me?"

She scrabbled around the dirt to find the quill, then lifted it for him to see. "We found you with this in your neck."

He looked down at it, confused.

"It's a porcupine –"

"I know what it is," he snapped. "What was it doing in my — oh." His head lay back on his neck. "Now I remember. That boy."

"Aedus," Alaysha said. "Girl, you mean." Aedus could easily be mistaken for a boy, she supposed, especially if she had muddied her hair up again.

Gael shook his head. "Not a girl. I've seen Aedus. I know what she looks like. There was a boy lurking around the doors. I didn't pay him much mind, but I did watch him a little."

"A warrior is always aware."

"Right. But inside the city, well, usually you can let some of your guard down…"

"But given the attack —"

"I trust nothing."

"So what about the boy?"

"He was drawing in the dirt just off to the side of the doors." Gael pointed toward the other side, and even as he did, was moving over to inspect the area. Alaysha looked down to see what appeared to be a small map. An X marked next to a horizontal line in a big circle.

"That must be you," she said to him, sticking her toe toward the X.

He made a thoughtful sound. "The boy was pointing my spot out to someone."

"Aedus." It made no sense, but Yenic seemed so sure she was just up to more mischief. She had a predilection for having fun at another's expense. She'd let Yenic wear the dreamer's worm just for a chuckle. Alaysha studied Gael's face, wondering what he might have done to Aedus to incur her angst.

Gael shuffled under her scrutiny and then huffed. "Do you think she did find her brother and is working from within to help him?"

Alaysha shook her head. "Her brother cut off her finger; she won't help him take over the city."

"Blood is blood, Witch."

Indeed, it might be to someone who had a regular relationship with blood. Alaysha's blood kin had sent her to kill hundreds of people in her short lifetime; Aedus's blood had used her as bait to attempt to murder an entire city. She couldn't imagine the girl remaining loyal under those circumstances. Alaysha certainly hadn't.

She had to ask the one question that lingered, regardless of how painful the answer might be. "What about Yenic? Could he have been involved somehow?"

A look passed across Gael's face that Alaysha didn't understand. "That boy? He wouldn't harm the man who was watching your back."

"Is that what you were doing? Watching my back?"

His unshaven jaw see-sawed back and forth as though he'd been caught at formulating a lie. "You took a dirk in the belly for me."

"Hardly; I just didn't want any of those men to escape." She remembered that some had, and that the ones he'd attacked had died gruesome, painful deaths.

She felt his hand on her shoulder and wondered at the way the touch could make her feel so small and so safe at the same time.

"You're brave, Witch; I'll give you that. But you are not wise. That boy wants you. It's clear, and if he's involved in this, he's better at play than any man I've ever seen."

She wasn't sure what to do with all that information, so she chose the least bothersome. "You think I'm brave?" No one had ever told her so. No one had given her much kindness, in fact, at least not until lately. She had the feeling it couldn't last long.

"You're the bravest witch I know." He started off in the direction of Saxa's cottage, weaving a bit, and having to find his direction constantly. Alaysha found herself following, watching his stride, thinking how many steps she had to take for each one of his. His shoulders moved easily through the crowds, despite being broad enough that he could have pushed each person out of his way. She had to hurry to keep pace while he seemed to be merely ambling along. She caught up to him just as she realized the impact of his words.

"Do you know many witches?"

"You're the only one."

They made it to the main courtyard and were heading to the cottage to the right of the keep, where

Saxa had planted a few lavender bushes. The smell crept across the breeze to greet them.

"Is Saxa a witch?" She asked bluntly.

He stopped short and peered down at her, making her belly flip-flop over on itself.

"Saxa is a born sagini."

"Sagini?"

"What you would call a shaman."

Alaysha was surprised to get so many words from the man and couldn't help pressing for more. She imagined the Carrion stretched out in the bathhouse, waiting for her decision. "Do you remember the man who flogged your father?"

"Corrin." The name was acid in the air.

"Yes," she said. "I am to decide if he lives or dies."

Gael made a noncommittal sound.

"What would you decide?"

"It would depend on how badly he beat me," Gael said, and his chin quivered, just a bit, then stopped with a defiant clamping of his jaw.

Her astonishment at her companion's guess might have propelled her to ask more, to find out what he knew of her youth, but she saw Yenic over his shoulder, coming out of Saxa's cottage, and for a moment she couldn't say anything.

He was holding Aedus by the ear.

CHAPTER 7

"It was you," she shouted as she ran past Gael. Alaysha wasn't sure if she was angry or excited, and she didn't care which emotion got the blame. She just knew she wanted to pick the little urchin up and squeeze her so tightly she lost her breath.

On contemplation, maybe it was anger.

"It was not me," Aedus said, avoiding Alaysha's arms and sidestepping very neatly away from Yenic who had by then let go of her ear. Her hair had been freshly washed and combed out; still, she found a way to make it hang in globs about her head and neck. Alaysha wonder just what kind of people Aedus's tribe really were. She looked so feral, almost like a raw bit of flesh that hadn't evolved, and yet still, there was a fierce sort of power about her that Alaysha hadn't noticed before.

Fierce was a perfect description if the girl's face was any indication. Best to approach this cornered beast with caution.

"Yenic told you what we found?"

Gael didn't wait for the answer; Alaysha got shoved rudely aside as the mountain of man swept the girl onto his shoulder and carried her off towards the center of the courtyard. He pushed through people, shoving them aside, striding purposefully.

It dawned very slowly on Alaysha where he was headed, and it seemed Aedus realized it too. Her shouts were piercing ones that set Alaysha's bare feet to a run. She didn't care if Yenic followed or not, but she heard him behind her.

"What's going on? Where you going? Alaysha. Stop. You've been hurt."

She bumped into a woman carrying a round of fresh bread and a basket of apples. They fell with a thud and rolled in a dozen directions. The woman cursed angrily enough but when she saw the one who had damaged her bread was Yuri's water witch, her face filled with renewed fury.

"Stupid witch," she shouted, and Alaysha felt the woman's grip around her elbow, trying to pull her back. "The deities have cursed us with you."

The woman yanked hard, twisting Alaysha to face her full on, and she lost the one last glimpse she had of Gael's broad back as it moved through the crowds. One last look, but she saw Aedus hanging down, beating him in the kidneys.

Alaysha faced the woman with a sigh.

"Please, forgive me," she tried patiently.

Rather than spit more at her or accept the apology, the woman's gaze narrowed. "You healed quickly enough for someone so injured. Part of your curse, I suppose." Rather than keep her attention on Alaysha's side, where she expected it to be, the woman stared at her tattau before she bent to retrieve an apple. She threw it with such force that it struck Alaysha in the neck and her hand went to the spot instinctively.

"Filthy tattaus. Mark of brown magics gone black." The woman scrambled for another fruit and threw that too, muttering all the while about curses and ill-gotten healing until Yenic drew close enough to pull Alaysha behind him.

"Woman, control yourself," he told the assailant.

She peered at him, pointing. "You're one of her people." She could have been spewing her own curses the way she emphasized each one of her words.

"I am," he said. "And she has been recently hurt saving your people."

The woman sent a glob of spit in their direction. "We wouldn't need saving if the witch was dead as she should be."

Alaysha tried to fidget out of Yenic's protective hold; when she discovered she couldn't, she had to content herself with peering beneath his arm.

"I want no trouble," she said, the old shame coming back heavy on her shoulders. The shame of having to veil her face in public, of hiding in her nohma's hovel outside the city gates until her father sent for her. She'd forgotten what it was like to be inside the walls again in such close proximity to Sarum's people. It was like living with a dog that enjoyed biting you when you least expected it. Saxa's cottage had felt so safe; she had been enjoying the time within as though she were like everyone else.

"Please, matron, let us gather your apples for you."

Yenic pressed her back. "We will do nothing of the sort," he told her, inching away discreetly. "Let her gather her own if she can."

With a glare, the woman reached for the apple closest to her. Just when her fingers went around it, there was a sizzling sound and she yanked her hand back, popping two fingers into her mouth. She sent a suspicious look Yenic's way. Alaysha eased out from behind him and he took her hand.

"Where is Gael taking Aedus?" he asked, and Alaysha almost couldn't say the words.

"The pillory in the courtyard," she said, watching, almost mesmerized, as the woman reached for her round of bread. The sudden smell of burned yeast met Alaysha's senses, and the round went black. She looked at Yenic who merely shrugged and pulled her along with him, leaving the woman to the sounds of sizzling fruit and the stink of char.

Alaysha thought she would have to kiss him later.

They found Gael just as he was closing the yoke down over Aedus's neck. The tiny hands were flailing about, trying to pull back out through the holes.

"You can't do that," Alaysha told him and rushed to heave the wooden thing back up. She felt Gael's heavy and callused palm on her fingers.

"Do not interfere," he told her.

Aedus started bucking where she stood, ramming the bulk of her wrists into the wood and yelling that she was innocent. It was painful to watch and Alaysha took the girl's cheeks in her palms.

"Calm, little one. You will not be here long."

"The deities she won't," Gael said, looking to Yenic. "You said this one had the quills?"

Yenic nodded, sullen.

"You say this is the one who shot me."

Again, Yenic nodded, and Aedus wrenched her face from Alaysha's fingers and started complaining her innocence.

In answer, Yenic went to Aedus and pulled at her tunic, reaching up under the bottom. It looked as though he was fishing around her calf and when he pulled his hand out, it gripped a pouch. Aedus's voice rose in pitch.

"It wasn't me, Yenic. It wasn't. I swear."

He opened the pouches and spilled out its contents. There were several porcupine quills, all filled with a purplish substance. In the midst of it all lay one long tube-like thing made of a hollow branch.

"Our Aedus has been playing again. This time with beetles instead of worms."

"Playing, yes," Aedus admitted. "But not today. Count them."

Yenic's finger went over the ground, his brow furrowed and smoothed. "Fifteen."

"Fifteen," Aedus repeated. "I had sixteen."

Yenic nodded knowingly and Alaysha couldn't stand watching the exchange any longer, not understanding what was going on. "So? Sixteen. What's the importance of the number?"

Yenic came off his haunches and faced Gael. "May I check your neck again?"

Gael twisted his head obligingly and Yenic grunted in thought. "It's purple." He studied Aedus and she squirmed where she stood.

"It may be purple, but it wasn't me."

"Yenic?" Alaysha said. "What's going on?"

"The girl made a sleeping potion while we were in the forest and tested it on me with her little quill blower." He nodded at the pouch contents that were still spilled on the ground. "She collected quills from a dead porcupine."

It was beginning to make sense now. "She used one on you," Alaysha guessed. Poor Yenic. Aedus so loved to test her warrior skills on the unsuspecting — especially when the unsuspecting was Yenic. She thought of the episode with the dreamer's worm during the night they had run from Sarum and Yuri, thinking they would begin a new life together.

"Let her out Gael, it wasn't her."

Gael didn't move. "She says she had sixteen quills, but she could be lying."

"I believe her."

It took a few minutes and a few dark looks, but Gael lifted the yoke. Aedus responded by kicking him soundly in the shin. Alaysha thought Gael would retaliate but he surprised her with a wide smile.

"You have courage, little one," he told the girl. "Rather like a cornered ferret."

There was no way he could have known the nickname her captor, and Yuri's favorite lead scout, had given her, and both Alaysha and Aedus shared a secret look with one another before Aedus kicked him soundly in the other shin.

He didn't so much as flinch, but neither did he smile. "Three insults would be the voice of war," he told the girl and scooped her up again, letting her hang over his broad back. His face was so calm, so good-humored, Alaysha realized that the large mountain of a man truly liked children. She couldn't believe he could be so indulgent and yet so hard. He strode off, Aedus bouncing unceremoniously against his back.

Alaysha turned to Yenic and noticed several citizens holding fruit as though ready to let fly.

"Looks like she was saved in the nick of time," she said.

"Looks like."

"Would you like to explain a little more?"

He heaved a tired sigh. "There isn't much more to tell. She's pretty devious with her little traps for me, and she does so like to set them. She had me dangling by my foot one night on the trek to my mother's."

There were two pieces of information she wanted more of in that statement, but wasn't sure which one she wanted first. Yenic decided for her before she could speak.

"Then there was the sleeping potion, and there was the bird that kept calling out to me pretending it was your voice. She taught it to say my name." He shivered. "I was glad to be rid of her, in truth, by the time we returned here."

It struck like a flash flood. "She has a crush on you."

He quirked his head to the side. "Besotted by me? Whatever for?" He pulled a charming smile and reached for her hand, captured it before Alaysha could pull it back.

"I do suppose I am a handsome rogue. Full of mystery. Charm…"

"Hog dung."

He quirked his brow and pulled her close. She could feel the heat of his chest, burning against her own. If only she could stop the questions nibbling at her spirit, she could enjoy the feel of him. Drink in the honey of his eyes.

She pressed her palms against his chest and felt the thudding of his heart. She told herself to push him away.

"Yenic."

He leaned in, obviously thinking that her plea was meant to encourage him. His lips were on hers even as she was trying to twist away, and instead of being gentle, they turned aggressive, hungry. He pulled on her lower lip and captured it between his teeth.

"I'm burning, Alaysha. I can't stop thinking of you."

She thought she heard herself sigh into his mouth.

Someone whistled shrilly and it was enough to bring her back to reality. She managed to pull away, and though the heat in her face was creeping down her throat, she worked to stammer out a few words. Accusations all, but words that had crept into her mind and refused to leave just the same.

"You brought your mother."

He looked like he wanted to shake his head clear. "Yes. Three days ago."

Her mind worked as she turned away. "I've yet to see her."

"You'd been hurt. I brought her to Yuri. He told her you were injured and mending."

It was true. She had been injured and mending. But something didn't seem right. "Yuri has kept her away from everyone."

"Or away from you."

Which point was right, she wondered, but she nodded at his guess anyway, and had to dodge a sprinting hound with a scorched and shrivelled apple in its mouth. While she wasn't ready to trust Yenic again, neither could she trust her father. It was entirely possible Yuri had plans for the witch that didn't include his younger, more volatile and unpredictable water witch learning to harness her power.

"How went the hunt for Edulph?"

He kicked the apple that lay in his path. "No trace of him. Even Aedus couldn't find his tracks."

Alaysha looked sidelong at him, and noticed that he wouldn't look her way. "She's a tracker?"

He shrugged. "She's pretty capable in the woods. It's almost as though they speak to her or something. Like she owns them."

"I suppose her people were used to living wild." She didn't know it for sure, but she imagined Aedus's people were more savage than civilian. "And she lived alone when she escaped Drahl. Scavenged for her food." It struck Alaysha that as little as she knew about Aedus, she knew equally little about her own people. She'd thought Yenic had those answers. No. She doubted that.

They were nearly back at Saxa's cottage, where she presumed Gael had brought Aedus.

"So we have no lead on Edulph and we don't know who shot Gael."

"And you are no closer to controlling your power than when I left you."

She sighed. "And I must make a decision about Corrin."

"That mound of dog shit? I should've killed him myself. What's to decide?"

Alaysha ran her hand along the bushes in front of Saxa's door and let the smell of lavender creep to the air. "I will have to take his life with my hands. Purposefully. Without a fight. Just step up and kill him."

Yenic shrugged as though it was a foregone conclusion and therefore inconsequential.

Alaysha reflected on the circumstances that had brought them here. Each time her father wanted her to learn her lessons that involved emotions, after her nohma had died, he took her to the cavern. Under Corrin's tutelage she learned to feel nothing. Sometimes for days, she was strung up in the bathhouse where she couldn't drink the water dry enough to drain even the lesser water from the walls, let alone the fluid from a man.

She wondered if a fire witch could set anything to light in such a cavern, with so much ready water the dampness in the very air coated the lungs with fluid.

"You would have had to kill him by hand," she said.

He shrugged. "How else?"

"I thought…"

He looked for a moment as though he was putting together pieces of the mosaic, and then suddenly discovered a missing piece. "You think I can bring the fire?"

She nodded. "The apples. The bread." She paused for heartbeat. "Those times when we were away from Sarum, from all this, Yuri, Edulph. You made the ashes leap to flame, you made the young fire blaze like old flames." She looked at her bare toes. "You kept me warm."

A slow smile spread across his face.

"You remember."

She couldn't look at him. "It was only fortnights ago; I can't forget."

He reached for her hand and dragged her to the side garden where the sage was tall and the daisies leaned away from them, pointing to a spot that was clear of herbs. A spot that was clear enough for them to sit, but camouflaged enough they couldn't be seen.

He gave her careful consideration as they sat together, his warm palm on her thigh. Something in his eyes wanted more but she couldn't tell from his face what it was. "What else do you remember?"

"Is there more?"

He touched her chin where the tattaus were. "We slept beneath the stars as you nursed me."

"You were hot then, too. Fevered. I thought you would die."

"You saved me."

"And you kept me from doing foolish things."

They sat quiet for a few moments before he spoke again. "Alaysha do you remember anything else?"

She got the quick taste of goat's milk, felt the strange sensation of a heart beating against her chest, of the feel of a quick kiss on her head. "A witch's memory is too long," she said. "Best some things remain unremembered."

He looked disappointed.

She shifted uneasily. "What will we do if we can't find Edulph? What if I can't control myself?"

"Don't say that. You will learn."

She noted he said nothing about finding Edulph.

"And what of the babe, the wind witch you called her? What if he's found her already?"

"If he'd have found her, we'd know by now."

"Is she truly powerful?"

He stared at her mouth. "As powerful as you, perhaps."

She reached out to him, and for the second time in one day laid her palm on his tattaus. They felt hot, hotter even than the rest of him. He shuddered and she caught his eye. "Your tattaus are of fire."

"Yes," he said carefully, but managed to sound almost despondent.

"You are her Arm." She needed to say it, to have him admit it. She braced herself for his answer.

His sigh came as though it had travelled a great distance. "Yes."

She ignored the churning of her stomach at his confession; there was something more important she wanted to know.

"How is it done? Does it need to be family?"

He didn't answer. Instead, he took her chin in his fingers and pulled his thumb across her tattaus. He cupped the back of her head and slipped his mouth onto hers. The kiss was so soft; she thought she would ache if he didn't show his hunger for her again. Then his lips moved to her tattau just on the cleft of her chin, tracing, she thought, each symbol there.

"Each symbol has its own magic," he said. "And each comes from the witch's own power. Until you can control it, you cannot offer it. Most witches come to their power after their matron is gone, and so they have been trained for many seasons already."

She could barely hear him, so soft was his whisper, so intimate and mesmerizing. So engrossed was she, so lost in his touch, all she could register were his words from before, that he was on fire. All she could think of was burning with him.

She closed her eyes and let him take her lips again, and she believed the tingling in her stomach truly was a fire igniting that would leap to flame if he kept kissing her, not the worry that he could be simply manipulating her.

His hands travelled from her face to her neck and cupped the back of her nape, pulling her even closer to him. Her stomach leapt as though flames had caught within and had begun to devour any doubts that wanted lodging there.

A nasty, guttural cough was the equal of a bucket of water to the blaze.

"If I thought I'd left you two young pups in heat, I'd have slung you over my back, Witch." Gael strode forward through the weeds and flowers, oblivious or uncaring of her unease or embarrassment. He nodded at Yenic sourly, but spoke to her. "You trust this boy?"

Alaysha didn't have an answer, but Yenic did. He stormed to his feet and squared off against Gael. He looked like a pup indeed, next to a large mastiff.

"I'm no boy."

Gael's smile was a crisp and calculated one. "Good. Then I won't have to feel any guilt at harming a child." He stepped forward almost innocently and delivered a crushing blow to the side of Yenic's face that was so quick neither of them knew he'd lifted his fist. Two moments later he reached down for Alaysha and hefted her into his arms.

CHAPTER 8

"Again?" It seemed this was all the man knew: pick something up and carry it. "What are you doing?"

He wouldn't look at her, just spoke to the air. "You have work to do, and not this kind of work."

"Put her down," Yenic demanded and Gael's glare could have set Yenic's blood to ice.

"Stand down, pup."

Alaysha squirmed in Gael's arms. "I was getting answers."

"I see that."

"You're ridiculous." Even so, her face flamed as Gael swept out of the garden and past Saxa's cottage, leaving Yenic standing with his cheek in his palm.

When Alaysha noticed they were heading for the Main Keep, she got nervous. "I'm not allowed there," she said simply because she couldn't think of anything else to say. "And I can walk."

Without ceremony, he dropped her to her feet. A stone bit into her heel and she yelped. "You are pretty much a beast." She sat down to rub the pain away.

"I thought you could walk."

She peered up at the handsome face, the eyes that reminded her of the water from the broad river that no one could breech. His face had become a storm of things, all of which Alaysha couldn't read. "I can walk."

"Then walk."

He headed again toward the Keep and Alaysha hobbled to her feet to follow. She noticed the increasing stares as she drew closer. Everyone would know by her tattaus that she was Yuri's daughter and his weapon, used to kill and bring victory of every sort to Sarum. They would also know Yuri made her live outside the walls and left her to her own devices when they weren't on campaign. A few women wore veils in a variety of styles depending on their tribal heritage. Some wore hoods. Some went nearly naked from head to toe. Sarum was such a mix of cultures that Alaysha often wondered how Yuri kept them all complacent in their accepted captivity.

The slaves were easy to spot because they'd been branded on each cheek with their owners' marks; the mere chattels and bonded wore undyed flax tunics shapeless and thick. Alaysha thought of Aedus and her clear cheeks and not for the first time wondered why Drahl had not marked her or Edulph when he'd had the time to do so.

She caught the eye of one man, whose cheeks were newly flamed from the branding iron, and she knew she could see fear in them, and the hint of hatred.

"I don't want to go," she told Gael.

"You don't want to train?" he said over his shoulder.

"With the witch?" She could swear her heart skipped.

He didn't respond and she stepped up her pace to walk beside him. She'd tired of the heated looks and she'd tired of walking obligingly behind him as a good slave would do. It was difficult to match his stride but she managed, and wasn't sure if he slowed just a bit to let her keep up.

"Gael, will I see the witch today?"

"We will see."

Being Gael and the tallest man, it seemed, in Yuri's army, being the brother of the favored wife, Gael had no trouble getting let in through the gate of the

Main Keep. Alaysha, even with her close kinship to Yuri, was different.

Gael frowned at the man who stepped into her path, barring her entrance. Eventually, wordless, they were both allowed entry and they strode unhindered to the outer audience chamber, where Alaysha knew Yuri dispensed justice when he needed to, planned his campaigns otherwise. What else he did inside, she would never know; in all her years, she'd never seen anything but war and more war.

Bodicca stood at the door, a match for Gael in height, her feet planted widely apart and her arms crossed over her chest. She had gained another bracelet of men's teeth, Alaysha noticed. She also seemed to have gained a new protégée.

Bronwyn stood at her side in an exact imitation of Bodicca's stance.

"They say the witch forgets her sisters too easily."

Alaysha didn't have time to rush forward before her half sister was in her arms, wrapped so tightly against her that she could smell the roasted boar in her hair.

"Where have you been?"

Bronwyn peeked sideways at Bodicca. "You see it." She looked back at Alaysha shyly. "I went to see you once, but no one could get near Saxa's cottage. It was barricaded for days. Not even a hound was allowed near."

Alaysha didn't want to think how Yuri had managed that. "You are taking the warrior's training?" She tried not to think about whether that would include Corrin, but told herself if it was Bodicca who was her mentor, she might be spared.

"Father says it's time and Bodicca is the best."

Alaysha looked at the woman, wondering if Yuri expected the girl to also learn the culinary parts of war as well as weaponry. "Indeed, she is," she said.

Gael, impatient, cleared his throat noisily so that Alaysha pulled away from her sister and stood. "I need to see Yuri," she told Bodicca.

The woman merely shook her head. Not so much as a glance Alaysha's way.

Gael pulled a dirk from somewhere, Alaysha didn't have the chance to see, and Bodicca grinned, rattling her bracelets for effect. "You have nice white teeth, man," she said.

"Go tell the Emir I am having difficulty training the witch," he said.

Bodicca snorted, indicating either that she expected a man to have trouble, or that she didn't think the witch worth training; Alaysha couldn't tell which, but she did nod at Bronwyn to deliver the news, and when the girl ran down the hall instead of inside, Alaysha realized what was missing.

"Where is the rest of the guard?"

Bodicca scowled her thoughts on needing more guard than she.

"They're not here, are they?"

The woman's face turned to a façade as stony as the wall she stood next to.

"Neither is my father here." Alaysha turned to Gael. "You both know he's not here, so why would you waste my time?"

Gael shuffled toward the woman and spoke to her. "She thinks coupling with a mere boy is proper use of her time."

Bodicca looked her over disdainfully. "She's young. The blood boils. Even in a witch, I'm told."

Gael's back stiffened. "The blood may boil, but my head must not."

The woman laughed low. "The boy is handsome."

Gael's voice grew angry. "Still. He is a boy."

"And you are a man, is that so?" The woman's tone sidled into a mocking one and Alaysha grew tired of the discourse.

"Can we stop acting as though I was elsewhere?"

Bodicca's head snapped in Alaysha's direction. "A witch should be elsewhere, not here this close to the Emir's quarters."

Alaysha sighed. "You know I'm his daughter. You've seen us together. You know I've never harmed him." Would that she could some days, but Alaysha knew, thanks to Yenic, that blood protected Yuri from her power. She doubted that he'd let that information slip to anyone else, though—even his trusted Bodicca.

She turned and headed in Bronwyn's direction, sick of the two and tired of waiting. Whether he followed or not was irrelevant. He'd brought her here, expecting any distraction would be preferable for the witch than an intimate moment in a garden. Why he would care, she didn't know, but perhaps he was right: distraction was a good thing. She'd lost her resolve with Yenic and she had to be careful. She didn't want to be manipulated again and if Yuri was right and three of the four witches could be controlled, who knew what evil a man could do.

She guessed her father was right that moment with the fire witch, and his guard with him. Well, she was here, and she was ready; she might as well get the lessons underway.

The corridor was one she'd not been in before and ultimately led to a stone staircase that felt damp and smelled of dead litter. Narrow and steep, it almost seemed cut into the stone of the mountain's base. Torches blazed every few steps and lit the increasing darkness.

She heard someone muttering and complaining above her, and then heard Bronwyn's clear, sing-song voice after it.

The curve in the stair gave way, and there, coming down at her were the shaman, wringing his hands in a bleached linen, a young page carrying bottles and jars, and Bronwyn at his heels carrying a wooden bucket.

"What have you there, little sister?" Alaysha asked her and Bronwyn glanced up sharply, nearly dropping the bucket in surprise.

The shaman spoke before the girl could answer.

"The witch speaks as though the Emir's good daughter knows her. Yes. But a good daughter doesn't intimate with the likes of such a filthy being, does she?"

Alaysha wasn't sure if the man was talking to her, Bronwyn, or himself, but she did remember his odd pattern of speech. She decided to say nothing to him.

"Did you tell Yuri I was coming, Bronwyn?"

The girl shook her head. "He's not up here."

Alaysha looked again at the shaman and realized something was going on. "Who is up there?"

"We do not answer to vermin, and yet she asks us as though she has a right, doesn't she? Foolish witch. Wait until we tell the Emir of her impudence." He bustled forward, taking the bucket from the girl. "I am done with you. Return to your post."

He twisted around to nod at the young page who hurried down the stairs, pushing against Alaysha in his rush to get by her.

Bronwyn looked to Alaysha for confirmation and when Alaysha nodded, the girl rushed down the stairs to disappear into the dark. Alaysha stood in the man's way.

"You have my father up there, don't you?" Saxa had said he was growing ill and that the shaman was working to keep him healthy.

"We will not deign to answer. Don't you answer. Oh no." He slung the cloth over his shoulder and tried to push past her.

"You don't have to tell me. I can easily climb the rest of the steps and see for myself." She was passing him by when Gael came up behind her. He reached for the shaman's bucket and peered inside.

"It's just water." Alaysha said. She thought it might be something worse and had checked it for herself.

Gael grunted and reached for the cloth, inspecting it. This close, she could see it was wet and brownish, as thought it had been used to mop up something foul.

"Come," Gael said. "You aren't supposed to be here."

"You brought me."

"And if you go up there, I will no doubt lose my head."

Theron watched the exchange with interest and when Gael noticed, he sent him scurrying down the stairs with a nasty glare. He gripped Alaysha's elbow; she pulled it back.

"Someone is up there. It could be Yuri. He might be sick."

Gael's gaze narrowed. "Why do you say that?"

Alaysha turned away. She didn't want to admit Saxa's confession. He huffed and reached for her again when she wouldn't answer, but she wrenched away.

"I'm going up there. I suggest if you want to keep your head, you pretend you don't see me."

Gael appeared unimpressed. His lips twitched and he swallowed. He seemed to be considering her words. She waited, confident by his demeanour that he'd let her go.

He sighed finally, and Alaysha felt a smile trying to take over her face until he scooped her from her feet.

She groaned and beat on his back as he loped down the stairs. She wanted to complain that her belly hurt where the wound was still healing, but she didn't want to give him the satisfaction. Instead, she sucked in large gulps of air and focused on easing it out, concentrating on breaths rather than the pain. By the time he'd made it to the bottom of the stairs and levelled out his stride she didn't realize he'd stopped until she heard voices.

His grip tightened on her thighs.

She heard a woman's voice, as gravely as rocks on heels, but definitely a woman's.

"This is one of your finest, I presume."

Speaking to someone, a third party, Alaysha realized, and that someone must have nodded in response. Gael sidled next to the wall so that Alaysha's head butted up against the stone. She growled and he slapped her legs in warning.

That was when she realized the silent someone was her father and Gael was trying desperately to keep his head. Awkward and undignified as she felt, she wasn't inclined to help him with the task.

"Put me down," she ordered only to be rewarded with a quick shot against the stone. She cursed and heard her father chuckle at the sound of it.

"Another one, Gael; do they never tire of being handled so?"

Alaysha tried to squirm off Gael's shoulder, but felt his hands pinning her tight. She opted to protest verbally, but he leaned against the wall so that her face got pressed into his legs. The squirming became more about getting air than about anything else.

The woman's voice came again. "I wouldn't think you'd have to woo your quarry that way, big man." She chuckled.

Several seconds passed before Gael eased away from the wall and Alaysha was able to breathe again. She gulped in a half a dozen drafts before she let loose a yell.

Gael ignored her and kept walking. She tried to knee him in the stomach, but found the muscles she needed to do so were still too sore.

She opted for quiet acceptance instead, considering what had just happened. Her father was with a woman going somewhere Gael was loath to take her. He'd purposely pressed her against the wall so she couldn't see, but surely he'd realize she'd know her own father's voice. Surely her father would know hers.

It struck her it wasn't Yuri Gael feared she'd see or herself Yuri would see. Those two things were second to the one other, critical issue. Neither of them wanted her to see the woman.

So who else would that woman be other than the fire witch?

CHAPTER 9

The seeds were nestled in a leather pouch she'd stolen from Nohma's larder. She thought the hide had once been rabbit, but there was no way to tell now. She only knew it contained kasha grain, a fast-breaking meal, and since she wasn't fond of kasha even with generous dollops of young honey, the six-seasons-old Alaysha doubted her nohma would care if the pouch went missing.

She poked a finger in and rummaged through the tiny, desiccated pearls that had once been four men's eyes. She remembered the looks on their faces as they'd died. She remembered the way their saliva tasted — of smoke and garlic and something unnameable that she would recognize later as ale. But on that day, two seasons earlier as a toddler of four, she'd not known and because of it, that was the most lingering taste of all.

She'd ridden out on her father's mount, hanging from a basket on its side, legs dangling from two special woven holes, her fat legs kicking at the air. It hadn't been her first foray into war, but it was the first where she'd be allowed to roam the field afterwards and see the power her father owned let loose.

The four men stood side by side, swords in hand, shields still on their backs. They had nothing to fear from a small child toddling toward them, naked and mewling of hunger. Nothing to fear. Nothing to protect their lord from. He would be settled into his tent just beyond, or so her father had said. He has something for you — a sweet bit of milk like no other, and when you are done you shall have fresh honeycomb from my own hand, he'd told her. Her father's own hands. And he would smile at her.

She'd reached the men, could see the tent beyond, the tents all around, horses, hounds. Even washer women boiling leathers in large cauldrons and taking down tunics hung in trees to dry. It looked so much like any other home, any other encampment she'd seen. Nothing special, really. No real reason for them to live and for her father's village to die, not when the village was growing and the buildings were being filled each and every day with new people her father cared for. No reason for these to live in the face of that. And die they would, he'd told her, if these men, this lord, and these washer women lived.

"Drink," her father had commanded.

She'd let her thirst go before the men could even kneel to help her. She tasted the mould from the earth beneath her, then the sweet tang of freshly drawn water: cold and crisp. The men in front of her had no idea what was happening. Why their mouths went suddenly dry, why their leathers and tunics grew loose as their skin shrivelled beneath it.

Alaysha stood beneath the gathering cloud until the men, the hounds, the birds and leaves and mould and earth were dry, and she waited until the cloud let go its water before she ran forward to be sure she had truly done her father's bidding.

The four men were so psyched they crackled beneath her hand, and one, the youngest, who had come to battle hungry and sick—she knew this as she knew each waterway of his body—was so dry he'd broken into pieces.

That's when she'd seen the seeds. Two each lying a palm's width apart. Her Nohma had ever told her a person's eyes were the seeds of their soul, looking out at you, drinking in your spirit. And now they were mere seeds, like the kasha grain she so hated to eat. What if these men laid down roots in all this rain? What if their spirits took to the ground and grew again? Father would not be safe. The village would not be safe. She scrabbled to collect them before her father could come and see she'd not done her full duty. She didn't want him to be ashamed of her. He'd boasted so often of her gift, what would he think if he knew she wasn't perfect?

She had nothing to hide them in but her fist and she clenched her fingers over them until her father came, as he always did, on foot. He didn't touch her or speak to her. He merely scanned the area, nodded, and walked away, and she followed him, holding tightly to the seeds.

And so, the pouch. Inside, they would gather no water. Take to no earth. Grow no roots. And buried beneath the ground in hard clay, no one could find it but her.

Four sets. Eight seeds that she could still, two seasons later, build into men holding swords and standing side by side if she wanted. A witch has a long memory, her nohma always told her, all the better to find water or know where it needs to return. The memory is the greatest gift, she'd said. Without the memory, a witch was worse than powerless because she had no control.

Alaysha was two seasons older now; this time, this first battle since the four men, would be different. She didn't care how many she drank from, she would collect all the seeds and she would remember them all as they'd lived, fully fleshed, fully hydrated: and remembering them would give her the control until Nohma could finish the inkings and she was a full witch.

A full witch in control of her power: seasons upon seasons after that, Alaysha woke with the phrase in her mind and a tear on her cheek. She'd worked so hard to bury all those memories and now they were returning. She well knew the difference between dreaming and early morning memories. The memories scoped into her pores and settled into her muscles so that she could feel again what it was like to poke through those eight seeds. She'd kept them secret for years until her father had seen her collecting them. That was when he realized her habit could be useful and ordered her to show them to him so he could count the kill.

And she had done so after every battle, each time, all but the one time she killed her nohma. Those eyes were the only ones she'd not shown for the count. Those seeds were still hidden, separate from the others.

She sat up to see Saxa already stirring something over the fire. The flames lent the only light to the room. Not quite dawn then. She had plenty of time to ride out to her cave in the woods just beyond the walls and collect her seeds before Gael came.

She eased out of bed, throwing back the soft linen Saxa had given her for the warm nights. Mindful not to make extra work for the young wife, she smoothed it over the mattress and barley pillow. The smell of lavender crept to her nose.

"Where are you off to?"

It had been three days since Gael had caught her on the staircase, and he'd kept her working from sunrise to sunset ever since. She hadn't even seen Yenic or Aedus, and she suspected that was on purpose too. She kept expecting a break so she could steal way, but even the meals were brought to them in the tiltyard—not even a league outside the city walls where the terrain had not been touched by one of Alaysha's early 'battles.'

"I'm off to get some time alone," she told Saxa who frowned with a moue both beautiful and dissatisfied.

"Gael will be here soon."

"I know."

"Then you don't want to disappoint him."

"I doubt he'll be disappointed."

Saxa pressed a pottle of warm milk into her hands. "Here. At least drink something."

Alaysha upended it and gulped. Even so, she realized at the last that this was nothing more than a diversion from Saxa to buy time. The door opened and in came the mountainous man himself and she knew she'd not get to her seeds today but would be subjected to more torturous exercises. She sighed audibly and followed him through the courtyard, ignoring the hissing she heard that came from those brave, or stupid, enough to do so in Gael's presence. Once, he turned on a man carrying a pig beneath his arm and cuffed him against the ear. The man quietly clamped his mouth shut and scuttled away.

At first, the sessions were mostly rehabilitation type activities: torso twists, squats, the types of things that would make her muscles scream before they would listen again to her brain. Simple enough, as any combat warrior knew, but towards the end of the second day, Gael began to incorporate the use of water. They'd gone outside the city walls, to the section of forest that she'd first fought in, and that had come back in the years since to a nice lushness. The river that swelled alongside the city was in full bloat here, and it fed the terrain around it. A well sat close to a rock wall, one that she knew travelers drew from, and the occasional country maid watered her sheep from if she'd shepherded them too far from their fields.

It was this well that Alaysha had come to hate by day two. She had to draw from it, carry the liquid a distance, and eventually drink it till she was bloated and nearly sick to her stomach from it. Near the end of day three, when she'd lifted until her arms were sore and her stomach muscles were taut in agony, and when she'd drunk enough she was just about to vomit, she refused to do it anymore.

"You will do it, Witch," was all he said. Throughout the whole of the rehabilitation sessions, he barely spoke, only barking directions when necessary; never giving praise, never encouragement. No casual conversation even came from his lips; she was tiring of his stoic manner and surly disposition that seemed more about something that warred within him than with Alaysha's presence. Still. She couldn't be too sure with Gael.

"I'm not afraid of you." She didn't have a weapon to hand because the work was never to be about combat, but she had tired of his bullying and more than that, of his silence.

He sent her a long and icy stare. "I don't fear you either," he said.

It was very nearly a challenge and she very nearly wanted to throttle the surliness out of him. If only she had her sword or her knife: anything to put a different expression on that face besides complacency or boredom, she'd give it a go.

"You should fear me," she told him.

He scoffed and spit on the ground at his feet. "Or you'll psyche the forest dry and me with it?"

"Maybe just you."

He regarded her thoughtfully. "Do it."

She blinked in surprise and ogled the bucket she'd just filled and he had ordered her to drink from, then let her gaze move sidelong to the left where a rush of flooded river bloated the mossy bank. She was soaked through with perspiration and Saxa's homespun flax tunic was filthy with wet earth where she'd tripped once or twice. Her belly sloshed with each movement, it was so full of water. She was exhausted. Tired of being the good soldier. Her fatigue spoke to her the way visuals and logic couldn't.

"You want me to try." The realization was so stark, her throat tightened on the words.

He merely shrugged and the stunning but rare smile made a quick entrance and beat just as hasty a retreat. It was answer enough.

"I won't," she said.

"Because you can't."

She knew he was goading her; she didn't care. "Do you have any notion how horrible this power can be?"

Again, a lifted, bored shoulder in response.

"You would be dead before you took a fourth breath."

His mocking grin drew slowly across his face. "'I'm thinking I have about ten breath's grace, and I could kill you in two." He reached into the leathers across his chest and pulled out a small, but sharp, dirk.

So. This was how it was to be. Manipulation, goading, and ultimately, betrayal. This time, the manipulation was for his death, not someone else's.

Would that she could psyche the entire world dry and be done with it all. She wasn't sure why this time, with a man who obviously hated her and would use her to end his own pain, she would feel the hurt all over again, but hurt it did. She had to swallow down the tears that wanted to travel up her throat and steal her eyes, but they clung stubbornly in a lump just under her jaw.

She saw him step forward and thought: this is the moment. He will kill me. There was no fear in her, only resignation and sadness because she knew it was entirely possible in a moment of primal instinct, the power would unfurl. She hoped her combat training would take over her body and the muscle memory of a thousand lessons would help her defend herself as best she could before that happened. Even as she thought it, she knew the instinct had already assessed the danger and had coiled just behind the training, waiting for the second she would have no last choice but to thirst.

He stooped in front of her, rather than lunging, and before she could jump out of the way, he had the bucket in his fist and the water flew at her in an icy curtain.

It was frigid, drawn from the deepest part of the well, and the shock of it nearly akin to a very primitive sense of fear. She gaped at him, then tasted sweat and tears, and the sweetness of new water. Now he would suffer. Once she'd pulled the easiest of the liquid, she'd pull from him. She'd snake into his tear ducts and down into his veins, his lungs, his heart...

She watched him collapse to his knees even as the mist began to gather in a bloated cloud above the trees. She could taste the wetness on his tongue, so intimate it could have been a kiss, so sweet, so moist.

She burbled over the mist of his lungs, bobbing on it as though on a jaunty river, his tears swelling in a happy gurgle. It might only have been two breaths, but the water was collecting.

Then she realized with a jolt he was laughing. Holding his stomach, bent over, laughing.

And that there was no mockery anywhere within it.

The surprise of it was enough to bring a sense of pure shame for her quick temper, her willing rise to kill just for the sake of her ego. So quickly did the taste of him leave her mouth, that she broke into a run and lunged for him, sick with worry that it was too late. The tense shoulders heaved beneath her palms when she touched him.

"You fool," she said as he peered up at her. "You could have died. I could have killed you."

He gripped her knees with his arms and pulled her against him. "I'd have died happy," he said. "Your face. Oh, Deities, your face. You'd have killed me a happy man."

Her hands went to his hair, twisting within it in her confusion.

"What are you doing?" she asked him, and stepped away before she could enjoy the softness of his hair between her fingers.

He slapped his knees and heaved a sigh, reaching for and missing the trailing movement of her fingers as they left his scalp. "Enjoying the first real laugh I've had in so many seasons I'd forgotten I could do it."

"No." She backed away, stumbling when her bare foot contacted a sharp stone. "I mean, what is all this?" She spread her arms wide.

He managed to clamp down a stoic face before any other emotion had a chance to lay on it for too long, but still, she caught it, and she knew.

"Gael, this isn't about my rehabilitation at all."

He stood and bent to retrieve the bucket, more to avoid her eye, she thought, than anything else. She waited for him to decide whether he would admit it or not. He lifted his head to the cloud that still hovered in the trees, growing darker and threatening to let go its weight.

"How long before it lets go?" he asked.

She shrugged. "I don't decide."

He seemed content with the answer, but moved toward the overhang of branches as though he didn't believe her. Within moments, the water came down in a hard sluice.

Alaysha stepped toward the trees, the water collecting in her lashes and marring her vision. "Gael?"

He upended the bucket in his hand and plopped it on the brown turf that had seconds earlier been lush grass.

"Tell me," she said.

"I could tell you I'm helping you to find a way to dry out that old Carrion."

She swiped at her eyes. "How did you know about him?"

She had reached the overhang and the rain eased off so she could just hear the pitter patting of droplets from the leaves hitting the ground.

He blew his lips at her question as though it mattered no more than the answer. She supposed it was accurate.

"You could tell me that was your intent, but it wouldn't be true," she said to him, trying to prod him on.

He plucked at a brown leaf, then another, and another until they littered the ground. "What if I told you I was just tired?"

"Tired?"

He stuck his hands out sideways so they both protruded outside of the tree overhang. "Of all this."

"You mean living?" Alaysha wasn't sure she understood.

"Living. Fighting. Feeling nothing… Feeling things that will come to nothing."

She examined his face, trying to grasp the full measure of his words. "You were trained as I was, weren't you?" She didn't need an answer, she knew it was accurate, but she waited anyway, hoping he'd say more, help her understand him.

"Very close to it," he said.

She wasn't sure how many seasons Gael had; she could guess thirty, but she couldn't be sure—his size had a way of inflating everything about him, and she supposed his age was just one of those things. She imagined a cocky Corrin trying to break this gargantuan column of man who would have been just as large as a boy, and found she couldn't. She wanted to ask him more, but he'd already stood and the moment of vulnerability had gone.

She followed him from the grove. The rain had stopped and the cloud she'd called was a mere memory. She scanned the area behind her as she walked. The damage hadn't been too bad; perhaps because of the gorging of water all around her, perhaps because she was full on liquid, perhaps because she hadn't let loose out of fear but of fury.

Or perhaps she'd just caught it in time and had managed for once to decide to stop it.

She couldn't help feeling a small twinge of hope that she was able to control the power and call it back, but she didn't have time to give it much thought.

Just ahead, at full tilt, her skirts held high as she came, ran Saxa. A look of pure panic filled her face. She was yelling, taking in deep breaths and yelling again.

And it sounded to Alaysha like she was saying Saxon had been abducted.

CHAPTER 10

Barruch had already been saddled when Alaysha gained the stables, Saxa close on her heels. Gael had sprinted off upon hearing that Saxon was gone and that his sister had already scoured the nursery. He'd shot off toward the stables with legs that moved faster than Alaysha had believed possible. His own mount fidgeted next to Barruch, Gael himself atop, fidgeting just as restlessly to be going.

Yenic held onto Barruch's reins, arguing with the giant with every inch of his body and punctuating his words with short jabs of the reins.

Alaysha stepped close enough to take them from Yenic and touched Barruch's white spot affectionately. He stepped away from her, turning his nose discretely away. She couldn't say she blamed him; he probably believed she'd neglected him and left him to Yenic and Aedus, two people he loved but who she doubted fed him parsnips or peaches, knowing his penchant for breaking wind afterwards.

"Everything is fine, Old Man," she murmured. "I haven't forgotten you."

He sniffled at her ribcage, and whinnied shortly. He was ever mindful of blood. For a warhorse, he was terribly finicky.

"This isn't the time," she told him and turned to ask what the plan was of the men.

The men's voices rose, Gael's blowing over Barruch's back to where Alaysha stood, trying to re-establish trust with her mount.

"You're not going," Gael was saying, to Yenic or herself, she wasn't sure.

Saxa's hands had begun wringing around each other as she tried to explain that she'd only gone to the garden for a moment.

"Did you see anyone?" Gael's mount snorted, almost echoing its master's disposition.

Saxa shook her head. "Just an arrow in his bed. Oh Deities. My boy."

In the end, it was Yenic who left on Barruch and Alaysha had to content herself with trifling things that could seem useful if looked at hard enough: chief among them collecting Aedus and sending her house to house, stable by stable, to question the good folk of Sarum. The witch at a woman's door would surely do more to halt the search than help it, and Alaysha agreed when Aedus said it with bald observation.

Trudging back to Saxa's cottage, Alaysha had a thought.

"I wonder if I might make use of one of your better linens," she asked Saxa, knowing the woman would offer it without question. Sure enough, Saxa produced from a fragrant trunk, a long slip of gauzy linen died the color of young grass. It smelled strongly of lavender and cinnamon, and another, odd scent she couldn't name.

It fit perfectly over her head with tails long enough to veil the lower half of her face.

"Does Yuri know Saxon is missing?"

Saxa shook her head. "There's been no time to tell him. I haven't seen Yuri in two turns."

"Is that odd?"

Saxa nodded. "When he's in Sarum, he always comes to me for his late night meal." Her hands began to coil within each other, and it was only then that Alyasha realized just how concerned the young mother was.

"You don't think Yuri has him?"

It was a touchy question but it had to be asked.

"Why, then, the arrow?"

Indeed. The arrow reminded Alaysha of Edulph, but surely he couldn't have made it back inside the city walls, and even if he had, why steal the heir? Why not aim to kill the leader?

It made little sense, but she couldn't think of anyone who would be interested in a frail child not yet off his mother's teat. She did know her father would be furious at Saxa. He had waited long for a male of his own body to train as his successor to his sacred Sarum.

"What of the shaman?"

"Theron? What use could he have for my boy?"

Alaysha had her own thoughts. Yuri was obviously ill, and the shaman and Bronwyn and Bodicca knew it, or were hiding it, or both. The evidence as to why was undoubtedly at the top of the parapet. She suspected the shaman had peculiar healing habits that were not quite so benevolent as Saxa's herbal healing methods; why else the secrecy about whom he was caring for at the top of the stairs.

What he would do with a healthy child of Yuri's blood to strengthen the Emir's, she didn't want to guess.

She'd had Gael to get her in the first time; now, she'd have to rely on her own cunning. Covering the tattaus was the first step. Gathering wild onions and carrots would be the next. Bodicca always fed Yuri from the fields if she could, believing the wild things tasted superior to the grown ones. Of course she'd let a poor harvester come beyond the kitchen door, especially one offering sweet bounty from nature.

She would need her sword, too, and pulled it down from its peg behind Saxa's fire pit. She wasted no time explaining to Saxa's curious gaze, rather, set about to fool Bodicca into letting her close to the kitchen. From there, it was a matter of sneaking to the corridors and up the parapet stairs.

She found she needn't have bothered with the basket of goods. Bodicca was nowhere near the kitchens, and neither were she and Bronwyn at her father's chamber doors. Instead it was a middling youth and two burly warriors Alaysha recognized from her last campaign. Further proof that Yuri was not within, but was somewhere else in his fair city.

It shouldn't have been as easy as it was to pass them by and the hairs on the back of her neck stood at rapt attention, waiting for some small draft of movement to give them away should someone come near. Should they stop her, or worse, follow her, she wasn't sure how she would respond. Sending the thirst was out of the question. Pulling her sword meant she'd have to kill. Neither was the right thing to do, merely to satisfy some curiosity. She realized the smartest thing to do was to take off the veil and let them assume she had a right to be there.

She smelled them behind her long before she heard them, just as she reached the base of the narrow stone steps. The torches blazed in their sconces, inviting her forward, and just beyond, as the stairwell curved, the torches were replaced by oil lamps that guttered in the draft of air that traveled down.

She sighed and turned to the men, pulling the veil's end and letting it trail to the floor.

The youth had obviously heard of her but not seen her before. The shock of seeing the tattaus on her chin, black and thick, was written plain on his face. The other two merely looked annoyed.

"They say the witch will eat a man's soul," the boy mumbled and reached for his dirk.

"Yours would be a pitiful meal," she said, and addressed the men when she saw talking to the boy would be useless. "I want to go up the stairs. I have business."

"What business could the Emir's witch have within his Keep?"

"What else, you fool, but the Emir's business."

The two exchanged looks even as the youth had taken to staring at the stone floor and clenching and unclenching his fists as though the movement could distract the witch from psyching him dry. She had to repress a laugh.

It took several heartbeats of staring them confidently down, before one, the obvious veteran, nodded his grudging assent. If the shaman or Saxon were there, these fools obviously knew nothing. She wasted no time questioning whether it would be revoked, and moved up the stairs as quickly and quietly as she could.

When she came to the only door at the top, with no further hall, she paused and waited, listening for the hum of activity that might come from beyond. Hearing none, she listened at the door, her ear pressed close, the dampness of stone around her smelling of moss and old earth. It would be foolish to charge in, even if Yuri was in there, even if the shaman was in there, even if Yuri and the shaman had Saxon by the heels and were spinning him cruelly through the air. He could be surrounded by his guard, or worse, by the Python-thighed Bodicca, and while Alaysha was confident in her abilities, she also knew in her healing state, that she was no match for the fierceness of that woman. In truth, she doubted she would be a match in any state. Many men were no match for that woman, and thus the reason for her being one of Yuri's most trusted.

No. Best she listen for the giveaway of voices or a light cough on the other side. She swore she could hear her own heart beating and she waited, and finally caught the murmur of a voice somewhere beyond the door. Perhaps to the left, close to the outer wall. It was barely audible, but she knew it wasn't Yuri's. It sounded like a woman's. Bodicca's voice, it must be.

Alaysha pulled in a bracing breath, tasted the sourness of damp stone and held it in her lungs. If she was going to do it, best she do it without delay. Best also if she enter slowly, with her broadsword on her back ready to be pulled into service.

She gripped the door handle and pushed, making certain to keep one hand ready to grab for the sword if need be. Bodicca was large, but she was also fast as a serpent. And if taken by surprise, the woman would react without thinking, not caring who was charging in.

The door swung open and Alaysha took in the room with gawking eyes, her leg muscles coiled for flight or fight.

Someone was in a bed, yes, and she felt the rapid firing of her heart when she realized that it wasn't Yuri and neither was it Saxon. Then she noticed a most curious thing about the person lying there.

It was a young girl, a teenager really, with long black hair and a swath of linens across her chin and neck. She could have been a scrawny thing beneath the blankets because there was barely enough of a mound of flesh to create a form.

The girl turned to her and Alaysha knew in the moment it was the girl from the day of the attack. The one in the iron-smith shop being scalded by boiling water. The eyes were hauntingly familiar.

Strange that a girl of chattel would be in here in Yuri's keep, being tended to by the shaman if the vials of potions next to her on the table were any indication.

Confused, Alaysha stripped the room into bare essence with her eyes. She stepped in and could hear a soft whimper come from beneath the girl's bandages.

"Who are you?" She asked, but while the girl's eyes looked as though they wanted to answer, the response came from Alaysha's left.

"You, apparently."

The sword was pulled from its scabbard before Alaysha could think, and she kicked the door closed so that she could see who lurked behind it. It clacked into its frame and left Alaysha open to the woman standing next to the parapet window. Tall. Hair like Saxa's, but so beautiful it made Alaysha's pride hurt just to look at her.

The eyes that looked back were mismatched: one orange the way a dying fire is orange, the other almost milky white. A ribbon of tattaus stretched across her chin.

Alaysha heard herself stammering and worked to get the very simple few words off her tongue.

"You're the witch of flame," she finally said.

The woman slid forward as though she were made of fire and was licking from stump to branch instead of scuffling along a floor made of stone. There was barely a sound. Seemingly, little movement. She put out her hand.

"My birth name is Aislin."

It was nearly too much to take in, but in a way it felt anti-climactic. Alaysha had waited and worried for this meeting for nearly a fortnight, ever since she'd heard of the woman's existence, and now the moment was upon her.

Aislin glanced at the bed where the scalded girl lay, her eyes in the full panic of a beast cornered.

"Poor thing," she said and perched on the edge. Her hand went to the girl's cheek, just above the bandages and Alaysha watched the young girl's eyes for signs that the witch was the reason for the panic. But no, the girl's eyes didn't shift. It was almost as though they had no ability to reason or had lost the power to show anything but the one emotion. Only when she looked at Alaysha did the girl react.

"I've done nothing to her," she said, thinking Aislin must have noticed.

The witch seemed unaffected by the admission. "I know," she said. "It's your father who has her afraid."

Alaysha breathed slowly, listening behind her, expecting Yuri to be at her back, but no. Nothing.

"She's not afraid because he's here," Aislin said.

Alaysha looked at the girl. "He's been telling her stories about me." It sounded flat, even to her ears, but it made the most sense. Yuri was forever telling people how powerful his witch was. Sometimes he didn't need to use a tool to make it effective.

"I do hear that you're a nasty, heartless killer."

Alaysha wanted to say it was true, but she had the feeling this woman would see through the lie. "You said this girl was supposed to be me."

Aislin's hand moved to the girl's hair, pushing strands aside thoughtfully. "She does look a bit like you. Don't you think so?"

She glanced up sharply and met Alaysha's eyes. "But not where it matters."

"The eyes," Alaysha guessed and the witch smiled.

"The eyes. Yours haven't begun to change, I see. So you are young yet."

"I have almost nineteen seasons."

"And a full tattau you don't know what to do with."

Alaysha made a conscious effort not to chew the inside of her cheek or to let her hand rise to touch her chin.

Aislin seemed to notice the effort it took for Alaysha to remain still. "It takes many years to gain the full ribbon. How did you come by yours so quickly?"

Alaysha felt as though she'd done something wrong and she inched away just slightly, lowering her blade, but not sheathing it.

"My nohma," she said.

"Grandmother."

"My aunt." Alaysha couldn't keep her eyes off the girl on the bed. "I didn't know any better." She looked the scrawny form over. "Why is my father telling this girl stories? What is she to him?"

"I suspect she means very little judging by the blisters she has on her chin." Aislin sighed and rose from the bed. Before Alaysha could understand what was happening, Aislin tugged at the bandage, pulling it up over the top half of the girl's face, and the girl let loose a sob. Her face from the bottom lip was covered with weeping blisters that all but marred her skin. It looked as though someone had rubbed soot into the sores or that she had gone under a poor artist's needle. Alaysha had to steel herself not to look away.

"It seems you had an accident on your way home one evening. Several men took it upon themselves to molest the temptress of the life blood and rid her of the horrible tattau that marred her beauty. I'm told the men were put to an agonizing death." Aislin let a cold smile spread across her face, but the look she gave Alaysha was a hot, angry one.

"I had no idea." She felt as though she needed to defend herself.

"Of course, you didn't."

It was all thoroughly confusing, so much so, that Alaysha lost the will to keep prepared and eased her sword back into its sheath. The weight of it on her shoulders grounded her.

"Nothing is making sense," she had to admit.

"Your father thought to use this girl to trick me into believing I was training his witch. It seems he doesn't trust me."

Alaysha shrugged. "He trusts no one."

"The mark of a great leader."

"You would've known she wasn't me if she was clear of the tattau."

"Yenic did tell me you were fully inked."

"And this girl was not."

It was Aislin's turn to shrug. "They made a poor attempt, but it's not so easy. It takes great skill, and a willing victim. And so the marring of her beautiful skin."

"You would have known eventually."

"Perhaps. After Yuri could be sure I wasn't going to steal you away." Aislin exhaled a soft chuckle that sent a tickle up Alaysha's neck.

"But you knew?"

The chuckle grew to a laugh that sounded almost like a fire crackling merrily. "A witch's eyes don't react as others. Has no one ever mentioned that you?"

Alaysha shook her head. She didn't want to admit how little she knew about her own people. "No one looks at me that closely."

"Or who can keep your gaze, you mean. They fear you."

Alaysha didn't want to answer that and Aislin pointed to the girl, who had stopped whimpering and was doing her best to stay calm. Her eyes held Alaysha's as though they couldn't look away, as though they were trying to speak to her.

"They all fear you, like this one."

Alaysha wanted to say that she didn't see mere fear in the girl's eyes, but something more like terror.

Aislin went on. "One witch to another, we know each other. You knew me by my eyes, yes?"

Alaysha thought of the mud hut village and the crones she had psyched dry. She thought of the eyes she collected, all different than the regulars. Smaller, perhaps, but not fully dried out. That wasn't the only way she knew them.

"The tattaus —"

Aislin held up her hand. "The tattaus made you certain, but the eyes held the recognition. You can't deny that."

Yes. The eyes. So expressive. So much the energy of the person who housed them. The center. Like this girl in the bed. Something so pitiful about who she must be, what she must be suffering. Alaysha wanted to help her. It would be nice to help someone for once. Instead of taking from them. Instead of hurting them. She thought about the mud hut village and the people within it that she'd annihilated when Yenic had escaped. She got a quick image of the crones inside sitting around an old fire of herbs and sulfur. Those eyes had all looked different when desiccated than the other seeds she'd collected. The first of a different set in the dozens of years she'd been saving and killing. She hadn't given it much thought then, but she realized now that those elders of power showed their uniqueness even past death.

Remembering the crones, and the deaths of the others that she'd caused just at the turn of the moon earlier, sent a shiver through her solar plexus. Just as she'd killed Yenic's sister, she'd also killed this woman's daughter — the temptress of flame in her own right when the time was to come. So Yenic told her. She'd believed him then; she'd believed everything he told her. So, did this woman know? Had Yenic told her as well, as part of his duty to her?

Alaysha found she couldn't meet the eyes that tried to hold hers. She took an instinctual step backwards towards the door and nodded at the girl on the bed who had inched closer toward her, nearly hanging off the edge, a slim hand reaching for her.

"If Yuri plans to swap her for me, he wouldn't be pleased to see me here."

Aislin advanced just slightly enough that Alaysha knew she'd moved, but so subtly it was a conscious effort not appear threatening.

And that was how she knew that Aislin did know. Worse, she knew Alaysha understood the breadth of the circumstances.

"If Yuri plans to swap this girl for you, best we keep him thinking he has succeeded."

Alaysha found herself nodding obligingly. The eyes that held hers had shifted strangely into a deep orange, even the milky one swirled within like flame on the rise.

"I can keep the secret."

"Perhaps then, we can see what we can do with you when Yuri is busy elsewhere."

"You mean—"

"I mean you do lack control, yes?"

It seemed as though there was more behind the woman's question than mere words. While her speech sounded forthright, and the tone was carefully comforting, the eyes, the expression, didn't move so. Almost as if the witch was seeking to see beneath Alaysha's skin, drilling down through her eyes, trying to read her as though she were a parchment.

The woman's daughter. Her mother. Her unborn granddaughter. Must be. The witch was trying to read what Alaysha knew about them and their powers and, she thought, she was trying to decide if Alaysha deserved to live.

Yet, something still coiled in her scrutiny that didn't account for grief. It seemed the woman didn't mourn what she knew she'd lost; what Alaysha had taken from her. And to offer teaching in return for such cruelty as Alaysha had delivered, seemed ludicrous.

Still, Alaysha so wanted it. Yenic had forgiven her the deaths; perhaps this woman had too.

It was a helpless shameful nod Alaysha offered next, and she felt as though a warm blanket had been thrown over her when Aislin responded with an indulgent smile. It seemed as though the witch would reach out for her and engulf her in a motherly embrace. Alaysha braced herself for it, both afraid and hopeful at the same time. She would've accepted the touch, but just when she believed it was inevitable, she felt a cold draft of air from behind her.

The young page who had accompanied Theron on his last foray into the parapet to treat the girl, the boy who had met her on the stairs, fumbled into the chamber with a bowl of herb scented water and a bleached linen. He met Alaysha's eyes, his own wide and afraid when he realized he'd walked into a discussion between the fire witch and the water witch she was not supposed to meet.

Alaysha opened her mouth to beg for his silence when she heard a snapping crackle coming from somewhere behind his eyes. In less than two heartbeats the bowl fell with a wet thud to the stone floor, and the flesh that had been a standing youth leapt into a flame so hot Alaysha had no choice but to stumble back into the room to avoid the heat.

No sound, no cry, no scream of pain came from him, he simply erupted into a length of flame that contained itself perfectly to his clothes and flesh.

"If it's to be a secret, it must be a secret," Aislin said.

Alaysha found herself nodding dumbly. She stole a glance at the girl on the bed who had squeezed her eyes shut so tightly that she had to rock back and forth to keep them closed.

Beneath the shock, Alaysha was numbly aware of the sense of something else besides the outrage of taking the innocent youth's life: wonder. Such power. Such control to contain the power to the one area, to throw it out exactly where she wanted. She felt the sure development of greed take root in her chest. She wanted that much control. She wanted that much command over her power.

"A secret it shall remain," she heard herself saying. "So long as the girl can keep quiet as well."

Aislin raised her voice, ensuring the girl heard her. "Of course you will, won't you, Alaysha?"

The girl who would be Alaysha bobbed her head up and down, never once opening her eyes, as if to say she'd been witness to nothing, knew nothing.

Aislin mumbled her satisfaction and bent to scrabble beneath her skirt to something on the floor within the ashes.

Alaysha didn't need to see what Aislin was reaching for. She knew it was the youth's eyes.

CHAPTER 11

Alaysha left with conflicted feelings. She had set out imagining she would find either Saxon or Yuri, or both in the parapet. She assumed she'd find the shaman there, performing some sort of twisted sacrament to keep Yuri alive that much longer. She felt sick that she believed her father capable of allowing his own son to be presumed missing, and even sicker thinking that he and Theron would use the boy for ill. Such was her mistrust of her father by now, and sitting just below that nauseous realization was the relief that she was wrong. Although what she had discovered would end up to her advantage, she was sick over the poor doppelgänger Yuri had placed in her stead, for whatever reasons she couldn't know.

And going to Saxa's with no further knowledge of Saxon's whereabouts made matters worse, made whatever elation Alaysha felt over her opportunities to train with Aislin dampen in comparison.

And there was still the matter of Corrin. The man deserved to suffer for the things he'd done to her, and countless others. She had no doubt that Corrin had trained Gael. She wondered how old he must have been and how badly Corrin had treated him to turn a naturally skilled youth into a stoic soldier for Yuri.

Add to that the problem with Aedus, and the fact that Edulph was still out there somewhere plotting his way in to Sarum, and into a wind witch's young heart; she began to believe she'd have been better off just doing her father's bidding without question. Things might not have been easier, but she'd care less about them. A lot less. Once again, she realized what a liability caring for others could be.

The sun struck her face as she exited the Keep; by her reckoning, it was just past the late meal, and she'd been inside since just after mid day repast. Saxa would undoubtedly be in full panic. She hoped Gael and Yenic had at least found a trail to track if they'd not actually found Saxon.

She watched people closely as she strode through the courtyard, keenly aware that any of the passers-by might know or have seen what happened to the young heir. She hoped if someone had seen they wouldn't be afraid to step up to her and let her know, even if she was Yuri's witch.

Most avoided her eye, and the more she thought about that and what Aislin had said about it, the more she felt a queer exhilaration in the deepest pit of her belly. The more she acknowledged the exhilaration, the less inclined she was to return to Saxa only to deliver bad news.

Her pace slowed without her meaning to do so, and she caught herself wondering if she could control herself now that she really knew it was possible. Somehow, she thought perhaps she had never been entirely sure control of the power was possible.

She thought of Aislin and the sickening smell of burned fat, of the quiet crumbling of a man to ash. It revolted her, yes, to see the flash of panic in his face, but so, too, did it excite her.

She couldn't stop thinking about it. She had been a child when she tried to drain Corrin. She'd been ignorant. Yenic had been right; she was young. Now, having seen what a woman could do with her power, how she could focus it, concentrate it, contain it, she felt bold enough to try.

Without thinking, her feet led her in the direction of the caverns, and past that, the bathhouse.

She couldn't face Saxa, but she felt more than ready to face Corrin.

The air inside the tunnel felt hot and humid. She could smell the darkness, the spores of fungus that grew in the thickest crevices. The faint stink of bat guano met her senses and she had to block out the gag reflex that wanted to take her throat. She told herself this was the day. This was the day she learned what she'd always needed to. What her father had always wanted. What she had to learn if she was to keep anyone she loved safe, if she would avoid being manipulated into doing what she didn't want to.

Today was the day she gained control.

She wasn't surprised to find him alone or to find the table beside the rack had been filled with food and then emptied. The remains of a cauldron of broth sat in the middle. A chunk of soggy bread half eaten by Corrin was being worried by a fat rodent who scurried away when she got close enough to cause it threat.

While his body looked weary, drawn, and limp, Corrin's eyes glared brightly at her with malice she hadn't known possible.

"I see someone has been sent to feed you."

He spat. "Two of Yuri's strongmen."

"One to hold you while you were unshackled, no doubt."

"The other to stuff wet bread in my mouth."

Alaysha reached out to feel the cauldron. It was still warm. "I remember," she said.

He sounded indignant. "You were never held by a soldier and force-fed inferior fare."

No. She hadn't been. She'd been untied three times a day for periods long enough to eat, relieve herself, and sleep. Her dreams then had been no worse than the waking life she lived.

"For months I hung here, not days."

He showed his teeth in a sarcastic smile. "So you've decided then, that I won't have months. Does Yuri know?"

"He'll find out soon enough."

"Go on, then, Witch."

He was remarkably calm for a man who was about to die.

"You've made whatever peace you can for a beast of Carrion?"

He closed his eyes, tranquil, unaffected; he made no response.

"You must have asked for some atonement from at least one god."

Still no response. She wanted a panicked face to meet her, a sly smile, a word of begging. Something. She stepped closer. "No one will save you, you know. Yuri has given me this decision. Your pot is still warm; the men will not be returning until morning to offer you a bit of hot, bland kasha. Maybe a pottle of piss warm ale."

She thought she detected a smirk, and realized she was managing to get under his skin after all. It had never been hard to raise his ire. She'd done it more times than a six seasons old girl should have been able to. He so loved to lose his temper. So loved to have a reason to hurt her.

"Yuri doesn't care about you. He has a dozen men ready to train his warriors. A dozen dozen. You mean nothing to him."

He peeped opened one eye. "And you do?"

"I'm his daughter."

"His witch. His tool. You are a soldier. Nothing more."

"Perhaps, but blood is blood." She thought of Yenic as he'd said those words to her, and knew it was true even as she repeated it. Yuri was her father. When all was said and done, she loved him, wanted to feel pride, not possession in her.

"Do you have blood, Carrion? Do you have anyone who will miss you?"

"I've never fooled myself into believing so. Not like you."

She laughed outright. "I've not once fooled myself into believing anyone cared about me."

"No? You've somehow come to believe your esteemed father has chained me here because he realized I trained you too harshly. When he knew all along my methods."

He couldn't have known it. He couldn't have. No man, not even the master of the tool would knowingly allow the things this beast had done to her.

"You lie." She felt her temper rise, the old desire to see him suffer, and with it came the ghost of a memory she'd worked hard to send down multiple dark tunnels of memory, so deep they couldn't be found. But the power had its own magic to unearth journeys even deliberately detoured. She found herself struggling to block off the exit before she could peer inside.

She must have backed away from him, because, when his voice came, it was farther away than before.

"Why would I lie when the truth hurts more?" he asked. "Think of it, witch. Remember. All those things. All of them, and more not done but sanctioned."

"Enough," she said. She tasted the mold and the wet leavings of bat dung. She wanted to retch as she let the power loose, and very nearly did as the memories washed over her like rain, soaking her psyche and making her tremble.

From outside of herself she could hear the faint sound of laughter and focused on the place it emanated from. Be done with it, she thought. She tried to send her power into his tear ducts, to his mouth as it guffawed, into his pores, but all she could taste was the sulfur from the baths and she very nearly doubled over in sickness.

"You're shaking, witch." It was a mocking statement, but it was true and she knew it. The sheer effort was enough to make her quake, but the memories that rode the tide of her power were the true reason for it. Seven seasons old. Ten seasons. Twelve. Each time she showed emotion this man bled it from her. Mocked her. Beat her.

Touched her.

"You can no more control your power than you could control yourself when I had my hands on you."

Beast, she wanted to shout. She didn't want to unearth those images, those feelings of shame and despair, the sense of impotence at the hands of another.

"You tremble now, as you did then."

"I trembled from pain and fear then."

"You were too young to know why you trembled, dear little witch." His eyes were on the mist that grew to a bloated cloud that stank of brimstone and stagnant water.

"I'm old enough now, Carrion, to know it as revulsion."

She clamped down the old images as though they were an iron door. She would kill him, she would psych the very liquid from his eyes, but she would not ever again let that memory surface. There was no need of it; it served no purpose.

She was a witch with enough power now to suck this cavern dry, and him with it. It felt grand to choose for a change. She would will it and it would happen. Of all the killing she had done at someone else's bidding, this was the first justified one. Corrin did not deserve to live.

She thought she heard a sound behind her: a shuffling, a short chuckle, even a half knowing, half speculative murmur. It pulled her back to the cavern and out of her power. She felt again the wet floor beneath her feet, watched the bloated and heavy mist let go the first of its contents.

Corrin still hung, untouched, as fat in the flesh with water as a leather water bag.

The sound behind her shifted to a voice. A woman's. The language was foreign, but Alaysha knew they were words.

She turned and saw Aislin standing there with her left eye blazing such a bright orange, flames could have been residing behind her brow. She crackled with energy, and Alaysha felt the air around her reach out in dry waves, mopping up the liquid on Alaysha's face and moving past her to where Corrin stood.

She saw the heat waves engulf him and move him ever so slightly like a soft breeze sent on the energy of a hot wind.

Corrin cocked his head, studying them both and resting finally on Aislin.

"You can't bring the flame can you?" He laughed in a sudden fit that surprised Alaysha. "It's too wet in here." He met Alaysha's eyes with scorn. "And it's too wet even for the witch to psyche it dry."

In an instant, Alaysha felt the brush of linen against her arm. She smelled smoke and tasted the perfume of a woman's sweat. Confused, she lifted her gaze from Corrin to the blonde blur moving at lightning speed toward him.

His face twisted from mockery to pain and in seconds he let out a breath of a sigh even as his blood spilled from his open throat onto his tunic. Only then did Alaysha register the knife in Aislin's hand and the smile of satisfaction on her face.

She noticed the woman didn't bother to collect Corrin's eyes.

CHAPTER 12

Three things kept Alaysha from speaking to Aislin on the way out of the cavern. The first was the grief of memory lodged in her throat, of all the things she'd suffered at the hands of the Carrion. The second was the humiliation of giving in to her emotions in front of anyone, let alone the temptress of flame.

The third was fear.

They left the Carrion where he hung; when she gained the open air, she made a flurry of excuses in the face of Aislin's careful scrutiny, then scurried away from the woman and hastened toward Saxa's cottage. Luckily, the shadows of dusk had crept upon the city and no one was interested in what went on behind the black curtain of night.

She wasn't sure what her father would suspect when his men told him of Corrin's death. More than likely he would assume she'd made her decision and leave it at that. She wasn't sure how she felt, knowing a man's death could be so easily dealt and so easily forgotten, but she did know she had meant to kill him herself. Did it matter the manner or hand that had done it?

More curious still was why Aislin had followed her in the first place, and why she wanted the man dead. She might not understand those things, but this one thing was immediately clear: while the witch of flame could control her power, hers was the lesser one to Alaysha's own.

She dreaded returning to Saxa's, and she knew Barruch was out with Yenic and Gael searching for Saxon. Where Yuri was, Alaysha had no idea, but there was one place none of those would be, and she made a steady trek towards the outer walls and slipped past the gatehouse into the surrounding forest.

Her own hovel was at least a hundred mount strides inching along the city walls, in a natural cleft of stone that offered both disguise from the outside by thick brush, and light within by a natural sunroof that let in moonlight enough to see her hands at night.

She wasn't heading there. She'd wanted her first four sets of seeds earlier; now, all she could think of were different ones. She set a path beyond her home, farther to the east where she knew the remains of a wooden shack still stood.

The years she'd spent in nohma's cottage, a squat, rough-hewn wooden structure with a fire pit instead of a fireplace, an earthen larder, and a wild garden were the happiest she'd known. Despite the weeks, and sometimes months long campaigns Yuri had demanded her to travel with him and his ever-growing army, and despite brief actual stays at the cottage, Alaysha felt more connected to life there than anywhere else.

When her nohma had succumbed to the power, Alaysha had never returned. The mountain and its bathhouse had been her home for years after, and only when she'd sufficiently learned Corrin's lessons and stopped grieving, stopped allowing herself to feel any kind of emotion, did she set out to find her own residence just outside the city gates.

In order to put a wax seal over those emotions, Alaysha had found it necessary to bury any memory that caused her pain. Funny, how the most painful had been the most pleasurable in its time.

She listened to the owls hoot in the gathering dusk and to the frogs calling out to their mates as she walked, mindful of the tree roots that wanted always to catch her bare toes. She wondered whether anything was left of the inside, and if she should brace herself for an unexpected piece of cloth or herb still hanging from a rafter, no doubt dried to a cob web by now. She chuckled to herself. Surely nothing inside had remained in any sort of pure state of recognition that could cause her worry.

A twig snapped behind her, some animal curious about the strange, solemn presence. She thought she might call out to it but decided to let the night have its own sounds and keep its own counsel.

She would have walked straight past the garden if she hadn't noticed the well, hastily dug and circled with round stones. The cover was long gone, decayed and rotted and gone back to the earth as all old wood does.

She halted and turned to face her home, and had to hold her breath for the abrupt pain that squeezed at her stomach. Home. So many seasons it was the only place that afforded any sense of childhood. The door was gone, leaving a gaping hole that had collected mud and grass. She stepped through thinking, even as she did, that she could live here again if she chose to. Forget Yuri and Yenic and Edulph and all the others who believed she was necessary to satisfy their wants, their needs. Like spirits at the darkest hour, those desires clung to the shadows and threatened to enter the light, never once taking the step forward.

Another owl hooted from behind her, shrieking in some protest only it understood. She stole a look over her shoulder and thought she could make out a set of familiar eyes in the darkness, just next to a copse of brambles so thick they could be strings of muddied hair. Then she blinked and the moment was gone.

Yet the hair stood on her arms as though danger coiled like a serpent intent on striking.

She'd get what she came for, yes, but she'd not remain. Something in the night wasn't right.

It took a few breaths before her eyes adjusted to the gloom, and it took a few heartbeats before she could stand without swaying. If she closed her eyes, she could see it all again, as it was.

If she closed her eyes...

Nohma's hands twisted in her hair, braiding, wrapping one string into the other. She was humming and the sweet fragrance of cinnamon furled into the air and curled around Nohma's neck.

"You have your mother's hair, Alaysha. Thick. Black as soot."

It seemed important, this information. It was something Nohma told her over and over again when she wanted to speak of her mother. Alaysha knew a story was coming, but there wasn't time to hear all of it. Her father would be here soon to take her to war. She hated war, but she loved being with her father. He was strong and tall and all his men were like mere pups around him.

"I have your hair, too," she said, reaching out to feel the softness of the black tresses between her fingers.

"Your mother's was darker, child. Black as your tattau."

Alaysha fingered her chin. "It still hurts," she said and her nohma's brow furrowed.

"Only for a short while. It will get better. Doesn't it always?"

"Do you think my father will like it?" It worried her that Yuri might think her ugly now that the ribbon of symbols was all colored in. She felt Nohma's thumb run across her cheek, even as a tear crept down her own.

"Why are you crying, Nohma?"

"Because your father will remember your mother, child, when he sees it is done."

"But that can't be a bad thing."

"Your memory is long, Alaysha, but seldom do we remember our birth. I had hoped you would remember yours by now."

Alaysha let her memory sprint through all the things it knew. It found days of killing. Days of eating and sleeping. It listened again to stories of an old war that spoke of souls living again to find vengeance. It even found a young boy with bright yellow eyes upending a vial into an open mouth, but it saw no earlier.

"Your mother," Nohma was saying. "Remember."

The girl had no choice but to shake her head. "You are my only mother, grandmother."

Alaysha stepped farther into the shack and settled on the same wooden stool she'd sat on all those seasons ago. It threatened to collapse under her weight, but she didn't care. The memory had returned and with it the tears.

That was the last battle her nohma had been with her. The last battle Alaysha stood next to her aunt and knew the happiness of being loved, or believing she was loved.

She looked around through a curtain of water that turned every shadow into a dangerous shape. She wanted to retreat from the memory as she had those years ago. She supposed she could thank Corrin for it now; it had spared her in the end.

It also explained why she'd been banished to the cavern and its bathhouses and the unending butchery of the Carrion.

She was weak from the remembrance, but she felt no anger. Only determination. A sense of justice left undone.

She forced herself to stand and move to the fire pit where she dug, hunting with her hands, peeling back a nail until she sat back with a sigh.

The leather pouch was ratty and rotted, but it was still there. Some seeds had fallen into the womb of earth and she fingered through them until she found what she was looking for: two seeds that if she let her memory, let her power, touch them, she'd suffer again the image of their owner's death. And that death was too painful to relive again.

It was enough to know how the power had managed to take her blood witch's life. How it grew past its limit to drain her where she stood.

And she knew it was because of that memory she'd relived out on the field that day, as she'd psyched the water from Yuri's last enemies, as she'd let her mind wander, as she'd left herself as she always did because even though she was a warrior, it bothered her to take the lives.

It was that bothersome memory of her mother's death that did it. That thing her nohma wanted her to remember about her birth. That memory of seeing her father taking a young mother's head even as the child she bore squalled its first breath. That memory of seeing her own father murdering the woman who gave her life.

CHAPTER 13

The shadows in the hut had deepened by the time Alaysha collected herself. She stuffed the pouch into an old hollowed gourd that rested beside the fire pit, and then she covered that with a blanket of moss she pulled from trees that surrounded the cottage. The gourd still had the remnants of a thong of leather pulled through the pierced holes on either side. It made a good enough satchel, she supposed, but at least she wouldn't lose any of the seeds she'd collected and put back into the pouch.

She thought it strange that any had survived at all left in the damp earth, but she assumed they were so desiccated by the draining that there was nothing left to help them rot.

She took a last slow look around the small place she'd called home and turned toward the maw of doorway.

Yenic stood there, filling the space, blocking off what little moonlight tried to steal past him.

"Last time I saw you here, you were a newborn babe," he whispered in a voice so painful to hear she thought she'd not make it into his arms.

He held her silently for long moments. She felt his heart thudding against hers, the heat of his embrace making her realize how cold she was. She said nothing as she linked her hands behind his neck and pulled him close.

It was all a lie, the things her father had told her. So much for his truths. For all she knew, he planted the mistrust of Yenic in her purposely while she was vulnerable and ready to hear nothing but how a man could betray her.

Yenic offered no resistance. The solid breadth of him against her pressed even closer. He tasted of old ale and onions but she didn't care. She could only think how she wanted to devour him, how close she wanted him against her, and knowing it wasn't close enough.

She kissed him with a hunger she didn't understand and when his teeth captured her lip, she gasped in relief of the pain she needed to let go.

He spoke only after both their hearts leapt the same rhythm; pulling away, burying his face in her hair.

"Sweet deities, you are so young," he murmured. "You've always been young."

"Too young for you," she said, guessing where his mind had gone.

He tightened his arms around her and lifted her off her feet, pulling her against him so she felt herself curve against him. "You were a baby. I was a boy. Young. I'd just got my first tattau but I thought I was a man."

"The bond," she guessed and he nodded, pressing his mouth into her neck.

"Your tears," he said and ran his cheek over hers; only then did she realize her face was wet. "Like these."

She could only think of Saxa's words so she mumbled them aloud, surprising herself. "Tears have magic."

"I'm bound to you by them." He took deliberate steps back into the hovel, carrying her with him, then eased her onto the earth. "I'm bound and, though I didn't want it then, I want it now. So badly."

She knew how he felt. Part of her wondered if this was all; if she loved him because of a bond forged between them so many years ago, or if she loved him because he was Yenic. Arrogant. Handsome. Infuriating.

His hands moved over her waist, finding the skin beneath her tunic and linens. She felt herself letting go, letting him feel her response. What did a bond matter when she wanted it just as badly?

She could hear her own breath, feel his on her skin. Everywhere his lips touched. Against her temple, her jaw, her ears.

She swore she saw the dead ashes in the fire glow with renewed life and lend enough light that she could make out the fine details of his jaw as he moved over her. He looked at her once and his eyes glowed like melting amber; then his mouth claimed hers again as though she could somehow quench his fever.

She thought if she never lived a moment after this one, she would at least finally have found peace.

When they rose together many lingering moments later to face the full night, she gripped his hand with hers.

"You can't keep things from me," she told him. She couldn't explain it, but she needed to know, even more now, that she could trust him right down to the secrets he kept.

He wrapped his free arm around her, pulling her to face him. "I've kept nothing from you that you didn't already know.

"I told you when we met that I knew your nohma. I came a few times to your home as you grew. One day I came but no one was here."

"Perhaps we were on campaign."

He shrugged. "Perhaps. Never again did I see either of you. The cottage went to ruin and we knew we had lost you."

She gave that thought and realized it must have been the Corrin years. "I was… Training," she said and moved so that his arms left her waist.

He gave her queer study and reached for her hand to lead her away from the cottage and into the woods. She followed readily. She wasn't certain she was ready to talk about the Carrion or the types of training he led her through. To talk of the man was to remind herself of his violent death at the hands of Yenic's mother, and although she felt renewed trust in Yenic, she'd thought it best to leave him ignorant of Aislin's part in it.

And his ignorance could not condemn him of foreknowledge when Alaysha saw to it that Yuri died a painful death.

CHAPTER 14

Gael was facing Saxa's cottage when they returned, peering in at his sister, who stood next to the fire wringing her hands in despair. The room smelled to Alaysha of new smoke and peat, masking the sweet scent of usual herbs that always pervaded the cottage.

Alaysha knew Saxon hadn't been found.

"Does the Emir know?" She asked Gael and his stormy look was answer enough.

Saxa was the one to speak, even if it was tremulous and soft, an unusual tone for the matter-of-fact woman she was. "Yuri came for his stew."

"Yuri asked where the boy was?"

"And asked why we hadn't told him."

Alaysha made for the fire, more to stretch her hands and think than to warm herself. The cottage needed no warmth; the air was as comfortable as that of outside, but a small blaze for a stew's sake was necessary. She lifted the pot from the hearth and hung it over a peg to warm, then thought of how Saxa worked at keeping her husband healthy through the food she cooked and wondered if it was the best way to Yuri's death.

Then she hated herself for thinking it.

She dislodged the thought as quickly as it came. It wouldn't serve to repay this kind woman with wickedness and Alaysha couldn't do that to her. Besides, she wanted to see Yuri as he realized his death was at the hands of his own witch.

She sighed heavily, thoughtfully, and turned to Saxa. "Where is he now?"

She shrugged. "He left."

Gael edged forward. "He's gone to gather the scouts."

"How do you know that?"

He planted his feet widely and folded his arms across his massive chest. "What would you do?"

Just that, she realized. The scouts had a knack for finding a trail and tracing it. The only person she'd not known them to find that they'd looked for was Aedus.

She sent a harried glance around the cottage. "Where is Aedus?"

Saxa spread her arms. "Still searching Sarum, I suppose, as you bid her."

"She should have returned by now."

"Sarum has many homes." Saxa put her hand to her forehead, and then seeming to realize that doing so made her appear worried and weak, busied herself collecting trenchers of bread and filling them with stew from the pots. She settled three goblets of ale on the table and pointed at them. "Eat," she said. "You three, of all, must be strong."

She didn't need to say that if Saxon was found and needing rescue, then Yuri would order his weapons to do so.

Alaysha stole a glance at Yenic. She was starving, and she knew he was too. She'd heard his stomach rumbling as they lay next to each other on the packed earth of the cottage. She pulled a chair and yanked at the top of the trencher so she could sop up the broth inside.

"Tastes different," she said.

"I added fennel seeds." Saxa hovered over them, pouring fresh ale that smelled faintly of honey.

Alaysha stopped chewing at mention of seeds. Seeds. She had left her gourd and the seeds from the hovel beneath the stool and now she would have to go back to get them.

Lost in the moment with Yenic, she'd also lost the notion to bring them back with her. Yenic seemed to notice her hesitation.

"Something wrong?"

She caught Gael's grey-eyed and suspicious stare from across the table and watched the way his expression shifted to one of careful scrutiny.

"Not at all," she told Yenic but made a mental note to return when she could retrieve them. Ever since she'd seen Aislin collecting her own seeds from the man she'd killed, Alaysha had the desire to make sure she knew where each of hers was.

Gael chewed his lamb slowly and sent a stream of ale pouring into his mouth. She noticed as he lifted his head back that there was a broad circle of scar beneath his chin that she'd not noticed before.

Alaysha touched her throat right where Gael's scar was on his. "What's this?"

He dropped the tankard to the table with a thunk. "Scar," he said.

"I can see that."

"Then why did you ask?" He grew surly again, which meant to Alaysha that she'd touched on something tender.

Saxa refilled Gael's tankard. "It's his training brand."

"Brand?" Yenic sounded horrified and Gael's bland look went to him.

"This from a boy with tattaus running down his side, ruining his skin."

Alaysha could feel the heat rising to her face. So he thought the tattaus ugly. What would that say about his feelings of the way hers ruined her face?

Yenic stood, obviously affronted at the words and she could have hugged him for defending her.

"I'm not a boy," he said, ruining the moment.

Gael sucked at his teeth. "How many seasons have you?"

"Nearly twenty four."

"How many battles?"

"Plenty."

"I have a number I can count. Four for every season of my living."

Alaysha swung her gaze toward Gael. Four for every season? Yet he was as unscarred and beautiful as a man who worked with his mind. Saxa must have been right about his natural ability, but to get through so many battles with only a brand? Remarkable.

Yenic appeared to think it less than so. "Your battles, though so many, old man, must have been fought in your sleep to leave your skin so pretty."

Gael's eyes moved to Alaysha's so fast she doubted he looked at her at all, but all the while she was thinking/remembering the moment he spent plowing through the assailants on the platform as though they were nothing but new, soft earth to his blade. He been marked then with blood and flesh, but he remained fairly untouched.

"Yenic," she murmured in warning, but it was already too late. Gael had stood, almost lazily, and squared off against him.

Neither of them looked anxious. In truth, they appeared to be looking forward to the inevitable.

The table soared to the side, Alaysha wasn't sure who had set it to flight, but it landed with a thud that seemed to coincide perfectly with Yenic's head butting into Gael's stomach. The fact that the younger man was able to get close enough to Gael to do so was testimony enough of Yenic's skill, from what Alaysha understood an Arm was capable of. Gael plucked him from his belly as though the youth was nothing but a gnat bothering an otherwise enjoyable day. He hurled the boy toward the table, then jumped for him so quickly she was amazed that such a large man could carry such speed. Yenic was gone when he landed, and then he was on Gael's back, only to be shrugged off. Punches sailed through the air, some landing with hollow thuds, but no other sounds came from the men. No yelps of pain, only grunts of effort.

She was torn between which of the men she should aid. Gael's face was unmarked, so tall did he tower over Yenic no blow could touch it. Even so, blood leaked from his knuckles. Yenic, on the other hand, had taken a great deal of massive blows to the face and his cheeks were swelling red beneath his eyes. She was rooted to her spot by the sheer beauty of their movement.

Saxa was not. She took the cooling pot of lamb stew and hurled it just as the two came together again. Hot, but not scalding, the broth sprayed over both men, hitting Yenic in the chest and Gael in the waist.

Both of them pulled at their clothing in instant alarm: Gael struggling to unlace his breeches and pull the linen away and Yenic working the tunic over his head.

Saxa passed them each a washcloth that she'd dumped into the cold water bucket.

"Why are men so foolish?" She muttered to no one. She touched Yenic's bare skin gently, nodding in satisfaction that she'd not done damage. When she went to Gael, he scowled as he stripped himself bare. He turned, raising his arms up over his head, slowly revolving, showing each inch of his flesh so clearly Alaysha would have been embarrassed at such nudity. Except most of his skin was crisscrossed with scars. He stopped, facing Yenic with his hands on his hips. Unashamed. Still combative.

"I am a katheel," he said, and his glance moved to capture Alaysha's. He held it as though he wasn't speaking to Yenic, but to her and no one else. "I am a katheel. A killer. I have been since I was old enough to take a foolish rattle to my favorite pup."

Saxa touched his arm. "Warrior, my brother, not killer."

Gael looked down at her as though he was surprised she was there and he shrugged. Then he reached for his tunic and breeches, his boots and leathers, and pulled them on. "Same thing," he muttered.

He pulled one last piece of bread from the remains of his trencher where it lay, knocked to the floor. He chewed thoughtfully, then headed out into the darkness.

It took several moments before Alaysha dared speak.

"A katheel? Killer or warrior?" It seemed important.

Saxa made a sad smile. "They mean the same thing in our old language." She said no more but set out to clean the mess, Yenic helping her sedately.

Alaysha inched away from the chaos, feeling guilty about leaving Saxa to her grief and worry, but knowing if the scouts had gone, so too, might Yuri and what better chance to seek her vengeance than in the whisper darkness of the wild outside the city. She scuttled through the courtyard and moved along the curtain toward the stables. She'd grab Barruch and find Yuri on the trail where she'd slip into his camp in the night, under guise of seeking the heir, and when they'd found him, she'd face him and, if she could, she would kill him.

She was headed to Barruch's stall when she found Gael, saddling his mount.

"Where are you going?" she asked him.

"I can't wait for the scouts to find my nephew dead."

"No one wants that."

He regarded her with something like tenderness. "You have your own battle to fight. Leave me to mine."

She couldn't keep his eye, and instead chose to focus on his shoulders. "What do you know of my battles?"

"Am I blind?"

She thought he must know about the Carrion and how Aislin had killed him, how she planned to assassinate her own father. She avoided his eye until he spoke again.

"Something isn't right about that witch," he said. "And you are too afraid of your own power to see it."

"I know," she said. "Both things are true, but you can't leave; your sister needs you."

She reached to take his reins from him and found when she did he grabbed her hand and put it over his heart. She peered up at him, confused.

"Are you really so young you don't understand?"

His heart fluttered beneath her palm. She could feel it racing. "I must have been."

His eyelids eased closed and he let his head roll back subtly on his neck, seeming to enjoy the contact. For several heartbeats he stood that way, pressing against her palm. Then he bent his head to hers and took possession of her mouth, giving her such thorough exploration she thought Yenic's kisses had been but mere play.

When next he opened his eyes, the tenderness was gone from his face. "A warrior needs a warrior. You could come with me, but only as my life's bond. Leave the boy. He'll bring you suffering."

She stared at him, feeling her jaw open almost comically. She was trying to formulate a response when a rustling of straw sounded behind them, where Barruch's stall had begun to smell strongly of too much manure.

Aedus stood there, her hair newly mucked into long dregs against her cheeks. Her blue eyes blazed bright in the torchlight.

"Thank your deities, Alaysha," she said. "I have news." She sent a furtive glance over her shoulder, then a bald scrutiny over Gael's form. "Can we trust him?" She stepped from the stall.

Alaysha rushed to the girl. "News of Saxon? Where Aedus? Where?"

Aedus took in the mountain of man. "Can we trust him?"

"What? Of course. What news of the heir?"

"Not of the heir."

Gael huffed his thoughts on his so-called questionable trustworthiness and launched himself into the saddle. "Have no worry about trusting me, little one." He pulled on the reins and nosed his mount from the stable, disappearing into the dark. Alaysha watched him go, thinking she should try to stop him but recalled the way he'd stolen that kiss and her face burned, keeping her from running after him. She found herself alone with Aedus. She turned to her, hoping the girl wouldn't notice how badly her whole body trembled.

"What's the news?"

"News of Edulph, not Saxon. I've been trying to get you alone…" The girl trailed off, watching the door with almost fanatical attention.

"Edulph?" Alaysha had a hard time moving from images of the young heir to the brother who had cut off his own sister's finger.

The girl nodded. "Yes. I know where he is." She lowered her voice and leaned in so that Alaysha could feel her breath move against her ear. "Or, at least, Yenic does."

CHAPTER 15

Alaysha thought she felt a bit of lamb she'd eaten turn rancid.

"What are you saying?"

Aedus closed the door to the stables and turned back to Alaysha. The look on her face was significant. It looked like she was telling the truth.

"Explain," she said.

"We found Edulph," she said. "Yenic and I. I knew his habits; I knew he'd return to our family home with his band. I took Yenic there."

"And?"

"And we captured him. I mean, Yenic did. Hand-to-hand. We snuck around the flanks. I used my darts to sleep poison as many as I could until I ran out."

Alaysha put her fingers to her temple. She didn't want to hear more, but Aedus kept on as both knew she needed to.

"By then, Edulph knew he was under attack. He called a fistful of men to him. And one woman."

"Greetha," Alaysha guessed. The woman who had flirted with Yenic on their flight from Sarum. She remembered her and the swarthy lover Yenic had been forced by Edulph to fight, as well as the head he'd stuffed Aedus's severed finger in for delivery to Alaysha.

She looked at Aedus's hand now, still scabbed and healing. Theron had done wonders to stitch it and avoid the green poison that so often crept in and stole a man's spirit. She thought of how hard Yenic had fought to get Aedus back and to keep Edulph from overrunning Sarum.

"Why wouldn't Yenic tell me?" It was a more important question in the moment than where Edulph actually was.

Aedus lifted her shoulders. "That's what I've been trying to find out."

Alaysha sensed more to the story. She sent Aedus a sharp look. "Why didn't you tell me?"

The words came in a rush. "I tried. I wanted to. Yenic and I brought him to his mother by the second day. We thought his men would follow us, but they didn't."

Alaysha's mind was racing. "No. They came to Sarum instead."

Aedus nodded. "They must have known Yenic's mother was coming here. They must've known." She said the second with emphasis and Alaysha gave it considerable study. Indeed, and they thought to rescue him when Yenic returned, but Gael had made short work of them. Of most of them anyway. Gael. A stark bolt of realization struck.

"You did poison Gael didn't you?"

Aedus hung her head. "If Yenic knew, he would assume I was trying to tell you his secret."

"You were trying to tell me his secret."

"Only because I thought you should know it; you shouldn't be kept unaware when the very person we are fighting against has been found."

"All the little tricks you played on him—"

Aedus nodded. "I wanted to be sure the sleeping potion worked, and I needed him asleep while I dug around in his pack."

"You dug in his pack?"

"I needed to hide a few quills." Aedus shrugged innocently and Alaysha realized how duped they'd all been at her protested innocence at the pillory. She had talent in duplicity, it seemed, and Alaysha couldn't keep the irritation from her voice at remembering she was the one who had made Gael release her.

"The hanging by his feet?"

Aedus shrugged. "That one was meant for Edulph, I admit. It was before we found him."

"What was the mud pie?"

"Laced with brimstone. To bind his magic."

"I thought you didn't believe in magic."

"My people don't believe. Edulph doesn't believe. At least he didn't." She looked deep in thought as she said this last. There was something in the girl's face that made Alaysha think Aedus had more in her secret arsenal than she was divulging. She wondered what else she'd have to get out of the girl before this was all over.

"But now you believe?" she asked Aedus.

"After what I've seen..."

Not so much, really. At least not from her. Alaysha had been careful to keep her power dormant when Aedus was around. But Yenic. Well, he might have pulled a few egotistical tricks himself. He was prone to arrogance in that regard.

"So why wouldn't you trust him, Aedus? What has Yenic done to make you doubt him so?"

"Just that he keeps the secret from you."

"That's all, and you treat him so suspiciously?"

Aedus's eyes seemed to shift color in the lamplight, like a shadow moving across earth. "Isn't that enough?"

Alaysha thought it through. It should be enough. It would have been before; a few moons ago, it would have been more than enough. Had she grown in those turns or had she merely become just another simpering woman ready to abandon logic because she loved a man.

"It was you in the dark tonight, wasn't it? You followed me."

Again, Aedus hung her head. "I wanted to talk to you alone, but you seemed so upset."

She had been. It wasn't easy realizing your father ordered such brutal training as had been done her by Corrin. Or that he'd killed your mother. "This doesn't help."

Aedus eased herself onto the straw and crossed her legs, pulling the heels in. "Imagine how I feel. This is all too much. I don't know who to trust anymore."

She sounded genuinely miserable, and Alaysha found she couldn't be angry at the girl. She was so young, so abused and used in her few short seasons, it was understandable that she'd think Yenic too good to be true.

Alaysha leaned to sit next to her, wrapping her arm about the girl's shoulders. She had grown, it seemed, in the few weeks since they first met. What had first been an undernourished, furtive and feral girl had plumped out in the moon's phase to become a better nourished, but more distrustful young woman. Or had the mistrust always been there? It reminded Alaysha again of how little she knew about Aedus and her people. Still. This girl becoming a woman meant something to her now. She'd been willing to kill the entire city to save Aedus from her brother. She squeezed and was rewarded by Aedus's head leaning against her chest.

"You can trust me, Aedus."

The murmur was almost sullen. "I know."

"You don't sound happy about it."

"I'm not. Something is going on that neither one of us understands."

"And you think I'm being foolish over Yenic."

Aedus sighed. "Why won't he tell you about Edulph? Why hasn't he told you that boy he shot was Edulph's man?"

Indeed. Why hadn't he? A niggle moved through Alaysha's spine, but so, too, did the memory of Yuri planting the same mistrust as well. Two very opposing sides of interest from Alaysha's standpoint, yet both managed to do the same thing. She'd sworn she'd rely on her own intuition, not the mistrust of others, back there on Saxa's bed, just after Drahl's attack when Yuri swept the Yenic-trusting legs right from underneath her. She'd told herself then that she'd not make hasty decisions based on someone else's words.

"I don't know why he hasn't told me, but he nearly died to save you, have you forgotten that?"

"No. I wish I could."

Alaysha guessed that having to question the motives of someone she loved was eating the girl up inside.

"I'll tell you what. We'll watch him. Just to be on the safe side."

The girl gave a feeble nod and Alaysha got up, pulling the girl along with her. "If something is going on that we don't understand, we'll just have to open our eyes so we can see better."

"And look in the right spots."

"And look in the right spots." Alaysha repeated.

"What about that big oaf?"

"Gael?" Alaysha felt a touch of regret when she thought about the large man. She put her fingers to her lips, remembering his kiss. Thorough, passionate; yes.

And so very different from Yenic's. While Yenic's kiss took possession, Gael's was that of a master leading his student, giving back as much as he took.

She felt a tug on her arm and remembered the girl's question. "Gael can be trusted without doubt," she said and knew it was true even as she spoke the words.

"But what would Yenic and his mother want with your brother, Aedus? That one is a mystery to me."

The girl shrugged. "I don't know. I just know they don't want your father aware that we found him. Maybe they killed him and they don't want Yuri to know."

"That makes no sense."

"If Yuri knows Edulph has been captured, then there's no reason to let you train with the fire witch." Aedus's face brightened at the prospect that she had solved the problem that was bothering her and could go back to liking Yenic again.

Alaysha thought about it. She'd learned in the caverns that Aislin owned more control, but far, far less power than Alaysha, and so it was possible that Aislin also owned some fear of the existence of a witch who couldn't control herself. It was possible that to teach her control would also take away the very real danger of Yuri using his witch's power to annihilate anyone, including the fire witch and her family. That might be the witch's motivation. And Yuri's? That might also be why her father had set a decoy in her place, thinking Aislin would be teaching a girl she thought was the right one, and thus keep his witch still under his control.

Whether or not it was the answer, it was enough to see Aedus content.

"You could be right, little one." She grabbed Aedus's hand and made for the stable door, intent on Saxa's cottage and a good night's sleep.

It was as good a rationale as any, and she would believe it if there wasn't one thing left to the equation, one thing that made her decide against the assassination of Yuri until she learned more. A thing Yuri, Edulph, and Aislin wanted. No. Not a thing. Not a territory, army, or city.

A person. An infant.

The witch of the wind.

CHAPTER 16

Both Saxa and Yenic were pacing the cottage when Alaysha and Aedus entered, and while Yenic halted midstep and grinned broadly to see both of them unharmed and together, Saxa was the one to rush forward, grabbing a length of homespun flax from a peg and throwing it over Aedus's shoulders.

"You must be tired and hungry, child," she cooed. "Let's get you some stew."

Aedus peered up at her, all wide-eyed innocence and Alaysha had to swallow down a nasty comment.

"I am hungry," Aedus said.

"Then come, let's get you fed." Saxa turned to Alaysha. "Gael?"

"Gone to search for Saxon."

Saxa made a humming sound that could have been approval or worry. Alaysha wasn't sure which. "He won't be back until he finds him, I'm afraid," Saxa looked pensive but managed to bustle about, setting a trencher of bread on the table and spooning a ladle of steaming lamb into it for Aedus, who began gobbling before she even sat down.

"And you?" Saxa asked.

Alaysha looked at Yenic as she spoke, unable to meet Saxa's gaze, knowing what lay deep within her spirit that she didn't want the woman to see.

"I'm going with Barruch tomorrow to the mud village. It has nothing to do with Saxon. I'm sorry."

Saxa turned to Yenic, and Alaysha knew she suspected something had passed between them as she spoke, but was too polite to ask about it.

"I'll fix you some fare for the travel, then," she said. "For the two of you?"

Alaysha shook her head. "Just me." She caught his protesting posture out of the corner of her eye and held up her hand. She hoped he could understand what she was doing and agree to stay behind. She had unfinished business at the village, and although Saxon was still missing, Yuri would assume she was off to help with the search. Ever his tool, she was. He would have no reason to believe she had changed.

She thought of the campaign of her first seed collection and remembered he never had given her the promised honeycomb from his own hand. It had all been a ruse to get her to do his bidding.

She had forgotten it, sure; along with all the other memories she couldn't bear to think about and had buried so deeply she thought them entombed forever. But she had recalled it after all; the same as she recalled his hands in her mother's hair as he held her head aloft, and dangled it in front of her nohma, cut away from her body, bloody, the tattaus trembling with the speech her mother could no longer form. And that memory had grieved her enough she couldn't protect Nohma when the power came.

Oh, yes. She recalled it. A witch has a long memory, all the better to bring to mind the pathways of the life fluid, how to ease in, ease out again, coax the fluid along, back out of the channels and into the very air, the pathways to her own pores, quenching a thirst so primal she could never understand where it came from. She remembered it and she needed, more than anything now, to find a way to control her gift, manage the power that he manipulated her with, all so she could end him and walk away her own woman.

The next morning she left Aedus with instructions to watch Yenic, so the girl would assume all was going according to what they had discussed. It would be a long ride to the village; it had taken at least seven turns of the sun to get there the first time and Alaysha knew she could use the solitude to mull things over. At least, alone with Barruch, she could find the quietness of thought she so badly needed. There was too much noise in her spirit to find the fulcrum of logic in it all.

The one thing she did know was that the village had started it and she had the feeling if there were answers to be found, that village and its collapsed mud hut would be the best place to start looking.

It ended up taking her six turns to reach it. She gave Barruch a few hours rest in between rides to refresh himself, eat, sleep, and regain his strength for another run. During the respites, she dozed and watered herself from the skin she'd brought, and ate from the packed basket Saxa had insisted on filling. It sent a wave of guilt over Alaysha as she munched on the herbed bread, knowing she planned to kill the man she loved, and she ate hurriedly before she could think too much. Then she lured Barruch forward with promise of sweet peaches from the oasis.

She knew she was close when the terrain lost its lushness and began to show signs of drought. In one spot, the trees were fragrant and green, begging to be stripped of overripe fruit and nuts; the next, the fruit lay on parched soil, dried to shrivelled remains.

"We're here, Old Man," she told him and he veered instinctively toward the west, where he would remember the oasis and the peach and honey scented air.

"Not yet. Not until you take me to the village." She jerked on the reins to point him toward the mound

Blood Witch| page 161

of mud she saw in the distance. He whinnied in protest, and she thought how much she was dreading the return even if it was deliberate.

It would be the first time she'd ever returned to a scene of battle. Something lodged in her throat that she would've named trepidation if it had a name at all.

"I know, old man," she whispered. "I don't like it either."

She let him slow to a walk, savoring the feel of a newly risen sun on her face. It might well be the last moment of pure ignorance that she could enjoy and she would enjoy it. There was no telling what she would find waiting for her, but she knew the magics there had been strong enough to keep Yenic safe. She'd seen the movement in the swirling spiral of smoke. What she wanted to know was if the magics were still there, coiled and waiting for her.

All three of the witches that remained: fire, earth, air, all elders of the tribe, all doing what they could to hold the balance against the fourth witch. Against her.

She hadn't known it then, that that's what was happening, but she knew it now. She knew it in the moment she remembered her father taking her mother's life. That memory ignited this understanding. When he took the head of the water witch to be, he gave that power to her daughter—his daughter. She was only one of four women destined with a gift all set to maintain balance. When she took their lives, others had to replace them. Daughters, or daughters of daughters.

She realized the fire witch had lost a granddaughter that day and would have lost the line if it wasn't for Aislin's absence. So the question was: where had Aislin been?

The witch of air delivered her power, at death, to an infant somewhere unknown. But what of the witch of the earth? Yenic had said only two of the three remained. He left out the third. Alaysha wondered if within the remains she would find she had taken the life of a daughter without knowing. Perhaps somewhere outside the village. The crones had seen fit to protect the lines by making sure one of them was elsewhere, letting the brunt of Alaysha's power take the eldest, the ones with waning powers, while the coiled and waiting energies sat ready to be claimed by a girl, a woman, an infant, somewhere else.

"Yuri must not know all this," she told Barruch. "He must know some of the tale but not all."

She took some comfort in the realization that her father, with all his seeming understanding, had missed a few pieces. And she felt rejuvenated in knowing she had picked them up.

She pulled in a deep breath as the hut grew larger the closer she got. The thatch of the top had dried and been picked at by roaming beasts and birds. She noticed some animals had returned: a hare sat chewing a tall sprig of weed, always the first grass to return to a desiccated area, able to find a crevice and take root under the deluge of flash rains that came after the power let go.

The hut itself looked dry and dusty and she felt just as parched. She'd not stopped in the last legs of the journey to water herself properly, she was so anxious. The leathered legs of the crone she'd left had been chewed and given up by a roving animal.

To her relief, there was no smell of decay, only that of hot earth and dried fruit. She dropped down from Barruch's back and let him find a place where he wasn't bothered by flies. She expected him to finnick himself to a place away from the dead and it was then that she realized there were far fewer dead then she left nearly a moon ago.

Barefoot, she stepped around the mound of earth and turned, hoping to find something more akin to what she left, and thinking it was very likely that the deluge of a flash flood had washed the bodies away.

There wasn't a single cadaver remaining on the battleground, and she might have believed animals or rain had carted them off, except, in over a dozen piles, waited cairns of stones, all in a circle, as though someone had done it purposely.

Someone had been here after her. Someone who had enough connection to the place that he cared about the bodies that used to be people.

Someone like Yenic.

She felt a flood of shame hot enough to compare to the heat of the sun that had started to bake her bare head. That she'd given these people no more thought than to collect the eyes they'd discarded, shrivelled and disconnected under power. How many people had she left so, to the elements, to nature, over the seasons of her warring. Too many. This one act must have taken him many turns of the sun to accomplish.

She couldn't very well unbury his people to justify a few answers.

"It seems as though we are thwarted, Barruch." She muttered.

Barruch dug into the earth with a front hoof, seeming to show how little he cared about the predicament in light of the more critical lack of peaches. A whorl of dust came from the ground and Alaysha watched it thoughtfully.

"You're right, old man." She glanced off in the direction of the oasis. "There's nothing for us but those things that come from the earth."

The elders still lay beneath the mud, awaiting exhumation. It would be an arduous task to dig them out, taking more energy than Alaysha thought she had, but she would do it if she could.

She had the thought that if she could tie something to the pommel, then tie that other end to the crone's leg, Barruch could move her from beneath the grave. Precious little energy from Alaysha would be spent and wasted.

"You're one wise beast, old man," she patted his neck and he eyed her with an anxious gaze. He knew she was up to something—something he would most certainly not like in the least.

"It's nothing. A little tug. Maybe just a little walk. That's all." She wasn't sure he was mollified.

He slapped at her with his tail.

"I don't care what you think. You have to do this."

He twisted his neck away from her to indicate his refusal, but it was too late. She'd already decided.

She rummaged through her saddlebags, knowing that Saxa had packed her a spare tunic and a linen sheet to stretch across herself at night to keep the bugs from crawling on and biting her. If she tied them together, she could make a strong enough rope. The leather thongs keeping her food basket closed would do to wrap the rope onto the pommel.

"No sense wasting time," she mumbled aloud, more to set herself to the task than anything else. She found herself thinking about the peaches too. She was famished and the fruit and cheese Saxa had packed was long gone.

It took more effort than she thought to get the material into some sort of rope, with a tear stressing the tunic. She ended up lying on Barruch's back, facing his tail holding onto the edge of the sheet.

"Go for the peaches, old man," she shouted and in a heartbeat, he began to plod forward, leaning toward the oasis, sniffing the air. When he discovered he wasn't moving as easily as normal, he halted, frustrated.

"Do you want those peaches or not?" Alaysha squeezed her knees against his belly.

He leaned harder this time, so suddenly Alaysha thought she'd lose her hold on the sheet. Too quickly, she realized the crone had come loose of the dirt and Barruch had begun to run. She fell with a thud to the ground, her breath stuck somewhere between her rib cage and her heart. She gasped painfully, hoping to get it moving again. Dimly, she was aware that her head hurt too, but that was second to getting her breath.

With effort, she tried to roll onto her back to make room for the breath she desperately tried to bring into her lungs. A sharp pain shot to her neck. So. She'd done something nasty to her shoulder too. Perfect.

She thought she might as well rest. It'd been a long morning in the sun. The heat was aggressively persistent and her mount had abandoned her in favor of a grove of fruit, taking her waterskin with him. Sure. She could use a bit of a rest.

Whether she wanted to or not, her eyes kept closing of their own accord. She'd even seen bright lights when she'd fallen, she realized that now. Must have hit her head.

The fact that she saw bare feet just in front of her with hennaed toes and insteps, with nails dipped in ochre, confirmed it for her.

CHAPTER 17

She must have hit her head harder than she thought; she came to and went out so often, and saw such strange things she doubted whether she was truly awake.

She thought she saw the pile of earth over the crones tremble and shake loose of itself like a hound shaking itself free of water. Then she thought she saw the earth open up bit by bit beneath the elder women and close over them neatly. The rest could have been clouds or sun or rain for as much as she knew.

The feet she didn't see again, nor did she see their owner's face. No matter. She ended up beneath a small tent erected from the linen sheet tied earlier to the crone's leg. It afforded enough shade that she imagined she felt cool, cool enough to feel as though she would be just fine if only the night would come. She couldn't remember erecting the tent.

Eventually, the sun blinked long enough that the moon saw its chance to shine. Alaysha was astounded to hear an owl hoot and the tentative chirpings of mice.

She eased up on her elbows. Dizziness peered at her from the corner of her eye.

"Oh no, you don't," she told the vertigo. "I've been lying here all day." She took the cloth from her forehead, damp and cool, and wondered when she thought to put one there. It was then that she realized the true nature of what was wrong. She had Sun Sickness. That happened to warriors who forgot to water themselves frequently or who worked too hard without eating. Made worse if the sun was strong like it had been, made worse because there was no shade in the desiccated plain.

She had done all those things plus taken a bad spill. Gone out of her mind, apparently, for a short spell. Thank the deities her warrior instincts took over and she'd done all the things necessary to get through the day and into the coolness of the evening.

She closed her eyes and breathed deeply. She could whistle for Barruch, but he'd be back no doubt when he'd forgiven her the slight to his warhorse ego.

She heard him, actually, just off to her right, munching on something that crackled much like a roaring fire.

Was it a fire?

She tried to twist sideways and saw with some elation that a happy flame danced a short way off. The scent of roasting meat and charred flatbread met her, and she wondered how she had missed it before. Yenic, it must be.

Perhaps she was still asleep.

She peered as best she could in the darkness, trying to seek out a form that would undoubtedly be hunched next to the fire, waiting for her to wake.

"Yenic?" She said.

"Not Yenic."

The voice, female with the rasp of a snake's rattle came from her other side.

"Aislin." Alaysha scrabbled to rise, not pleased about appearing weak in front of Yenic's mother—a woman who could set her to cinder if she wanted, if she ached for the daughter buried beneath one of the Cairns just yonder.

A soft chuckle met her movements.

"Take your time, Alaysha."

Alaysha gripped the damp cloth that had been lying on her forehead. "Thank you," she said holding it out.

Aislin looked at it, but shook her head. "You might need it. Are you hungry?"

Alaysha found herself nodding eagerly, the taste of the meat already on her palate. "Yenic told you I was here."

Aislin swept her arm in the direction of the blaze as she walked toward the fire. The flames beneath a spitted hare fell flat while the rest of the fire blazed on. She reached for the handle of the spit and pulled it from the fire, laying the meat on a flat rock. As soon as the spit was removed, the flames leapt back into place.

"That's wonderful," Alaysha said and the woman's grin came easily.

"You don't have such control?"

Alaysha shook her head, not trusting her mouth to form words over the flood of hunger.

"No matter."

The way Aislin said it sounded to Alaysha as though it almost carried a hint of relief. The sun sickness again, she supposed. She watched the woman tear a leg from the hare and wrap it in cloth, then she laid it on the ground for Alaysha to retrieve. She could swear as the cloth met earth that a spark shot from Aislin's fingers.

The meat had just enough smoke within to make it succulent. The juices, hot and oily, ran down her chin. Aislin placed a few strips delicately into the middle of a flat of bread she'd baked on a stone, then wrapped the ends in and nibbled at it.

Alaysha felt very much like a savage, and indeed the tender swelling of her head and the remains of sun sickness left her staring, docile and dumb, across the flames and into the depths of space beyond. She could swear she saw the bright gaze of an animal out there. Or was it a pair of fireflies? It was too hard to tell in the dark.

She chewed sombrely, lost in her thoughts, and in the mesmerizing dance of flames, with the animal's gaze just beyond, she thought she could find peace. She tasted strange spices in the meat, spices that seemed more to do with rituals than cooking, spices her nohma had mixed for her and spread across her firepit every new moonphase. A moon very much like this one, torn into the blanket of night like a fingernail. And now she thought it, she smelled other things too.

Things that took her into the grip of memory and made her walk there, choosing paths from the maze of images as though she were selecting choice nuts from a tree. Each path, though the images were different, seemed to lead to the same place, and that place was sitting right next to the fire with Aislin next to her, those eyes blinking at her from across the flames, her nohma's voice in her ear whispering of a place called Etlantium.

She could have lulled herself to sleep as she sat there, wrapped in the miasma of smells and memories, but Aislin prodded her, commanding attention.

"The fire has magic, does it not?"

"Yes."

"What do you see in the flames, Alaysha?"

"My nohma's fire."

"Nothing else?"

"Myself."

"As you are now?"

"As I was."

"And how were you, Alaysha?" Aislin's voice held a tension that reminded Alaysha of a panther set to strike. She knew she had to respond, she couldn't help but respond, but she found herself struggling for the words.

Words were in there, somewhere, that could explain what she saw, but she had to work to find them. She could see her nohma's fire pit so clearly, hear her voice telling her of Etlantium, weaving stories of old wars and heroes. Fairytales to set a young girl's fancies ablaze with excitement and wash them down with the sobering taste of heroines killed and lovers lost. How to distill that? How to distill all those images that came before it, of her wearing skin of a different shade, of hearing her name pronounced with different letters. How to capture it. She just didn't know how.

"Etlantium," she said and felt Aislin move closer. She could smell myrrh on Aislin's skin and Alaysha's tattaus and skin tingled as though they had been touched. Another scent came too, one that began to overtake that of myrrh, and yes, frankincense now she thought about it, brimstone. She smelled brimstone and the eyes from across the fire blazed brighter as she understood what the smell was. She was about to reach out to those eyes, one eye really, floating there in the darkness beyond the blaze, but a high-pitched whinny came from somewhere to her side and she realized Barruch had finally decided to seek her out.

She took a deep, cleansing breath and eased herself to her feet. Her side still ached where she'd fallen, and she was most assuredly still dizzy, but the food made her feel better.

She turned to Aislin, feeling oddly refreshed.

"I don't think I've tasted better fire-roasted hare."

Aislin's face looked guarded in the firelight, but then she smiled and the movement seemed to adjust the shadows.

"Yenic always tells me the same."

"He didn't come with you." Alaysha couldn't help the disappointment in her voice.

"I only came to give you a message."

"What is it?"

"Don't come to Sarum until you can bring the rain with you."

Alaysha felt her brow furrow in confusion. "Come?"

Aislin moved closer to the fire, ignoring Alaysha's question. Beyond, the eyes still glowed, and Alaysha could swear they held Aislin mesmerized until she spoke again in a foreign tongue and the blinking of the gaze past the fire went dark. The brooding tension of the place lifted but Alaysha felt no less anxious.

"Don't return." Aislin could have been chastising an errant child.

"I won't."

Aislin folded her arms across her chest and in the closeness of the flame she almost seemed hollow and faded. "Not until you can bring the water rather than take it."

Taking was easy. Alaysha had never thought about bringing it; her father had repeatedly said she could, but she always thought the power did what it willed once it had left her.

Recalling Yuri brought a sour taste to Alaysha's mouth. Would that she could control the power long enough to bring him the death he deserved. She couldn't take the water from him, but she could drown him with it if she brought enough. For the things he'd done, for the things he'd made her do, for what he owned because of her. She felt the hatred burning inside.

"I will bring the rain," she said and Aislin moved closer still to the fire, stepping close enough that Alaysha thought to cry out in warning, but then the woman became flame and then smoke, and Alaysha's head hurt so much she had to hold onto it.

She reached down for the damp cloth where she'd dropped it. It had cooled considerably and felt lovely against her skin. She pressed it against her eyes, thinking how decadent it felt to close them. How decadent it would feel to lie beneath the linen tent and sleep.

The fire had died down anyway; it barely looked as though it had blazed at all.

With heavy feet, she trudged to where she knew the bed waited in the dark. She felt her leg brush against it and climbed beneath, stretching out on the side that wasn't so sore. She took one last look into the shadows where the animal sat crouched in the darkness and decided if it had been a beast of prey, it would have struck by now.

She listened for Barruch, who would sound the alarm of any dangerous scent. She heard him letting go wind and smiled to herself.

She'd let herself sleep and come morning, she'd work to bring the rain. Yes. And then she would head back to Sarum and claim the teaching the fire witch offered. She had offered it, had she not? Alaysha couldn't remember, but she had the distinct impression that if she could bring rain rather than take it, that Aislin would know she was ready.

Barruch's breathing fell to a steady rhythm that acted as a lullaby; Alaysha could no more keep her breath from matching his than she could keep her heart from beating. She inhaled, content, and kept her gaze, mesmerized, at the eyes of the animal that blinked at her from across the darkness.

Strange how it sounded as though it was weeping.

CHAPTER 18

A spray of water woke her and Alaysha opened her eyes to a wide, wet, black nose in her face. Barruch's chin whiskers tickled her throat, and his eyes blinked impatiently at her.

He blew another spray of spittle at her face.

"There are better ways to wake a girl," she complained, but she rolled to her good side and made the attempt to get her feet. She wavered for a spell before she felt solid enough to take a few steps.

The remains of a fire sat smoldering to her right. So. Aislin had been there. Alaysha was afraid the whole experience had been the result of too much sun and a good wallop on a soft skull.

Bring the rain, Aislin had said. It seemed an insurmountable task, when it was too opposite the things she'd always done so naturally, the things she'd done to kill.

She surveyed the area, walking barefoot across the packed earth, taking note where small clumps of grass dared take root. A cactus that had once been as large as a man had fallen over, but it sprouted a thin arm from the side that faced the sun. It seemed some life had managed to cling to existence when the flood came. The land still looked ruined, but at least it was coming back. Given time, perhaps three or four seasons, there might be enough life to support a thin tree, perhaps a bird or two, but she doubted fruit bearing foliage would ever return. The soil was simply too parched.

Barruch clomped along with her, avoiding the cairns and sidestepping neatly to the left when she bent to inspect the mounds of rock. She should have asked

Aislin if Yenic had put his sister in a marked or unmarked pile, but then she supposed he would have no need of such markings to remember which was hers.

To bring water to this landscape would require a witch with incredible power, she realized. If there was some liquid somewhere, perhaps she could manage it, but the amount she had pulled from it had been so great it had collected and released in a flash flood that ran across the land too fast to seep in.

She glanced sidelong at Barruch.

"I don't think it can be done, old man."

He gave her a baleful stare that she thought could be a look of challenge.

"You might be better off back at the oasis. Just in case."

He pressed his nose beneath her hand and she stroked it affectionately, letting her palm linger on his white patch.

"Go, my man," she said, then slapped his rump. He whinnied in protest.

"Go, you stinking bag of wind. What are you waiting for?"

He took a side-step but didn't canter off. She placed her hands on her hips and faced him. "You can't stay. You know that."

She slapped him harder and he reached around and nipped her on the arm. She yelped in surprise and smacked him again.

"What was that for? You're acting so strange. Peaches. There're peaches. Go."

This time he did go. He shot off as though he couldn't wait to get away. She knew she'd hurt his feelings; he was such a sensitive beast, that one. She watched the dust whorl behind him. Listened to the sound of his hooves beating earth. She told herself she'd make it up to him, take him for a good run in a soft plain when she could, when this was all over.

She sucked in a bolstering draft of air. How should she go about it, should she try to think of the river that wound past her father's city, should she imagine the clouds pulling together into one large billowing mass?

Giving to instead of taking from. That might not be something she could do. But she had to try.

For long moments she stood, afraid to let the power so much as seek out a droplet of dew. In those long moments she counted her heart beats, thinking it would distract her enough to avoid doing the usual sniffing divination she always did before letting the power take her. She always went somewhere when the gift came. It came; she went. Perhaps that was the reason she had no control; she wasn't truly and fully present when she psyched. The guilt of killing forced her to distance herself.

No matter how long she stood, nothing happened. She remained on her feet for so long she got a cramp in her calf and had to bend to rub it out.

She knew then that she'd have to give in. She'd have to back off and let the psyching come forward, but she wouldn't travel the paths, no. Not into the pores of grass or that short bit of cactus. There wasn't enough water in any of it to take anyway. There wasn't enough water anywhere to pull from. She wasn't sure why she was so nervous; no water existed near enough to thirst from. No water except the broad body to the east, the river so wide they said it had no other side. So wide it had no end and so deep it had no bottom.

She felt hot, and she felt so cold, she could swear she had fallen into that broad river. A curtain of water could have cascaded over her in those seconds she felt so wet. It was then she knew she had done it.

She had brought the rain.

And no finicky, sparse drizzle either, but a deluge usually only accompanied by wind and lightning, and usually only in the rainy season, during the rare times when the air was too hot to breathe.

A rain so heavy she could barely see. So hard it landed on the earth and sent plumes of dust into the air until the dust became mud and the water started to collect in the hollow places.

A rain so fierce it gathered itself into a river much the same as the one with no end and no bottom.

A rain so commanding it raised the level of panic within her chest. Yes. She brought the rain, all right, but she brought too much, too soon, too hard, and she had no idea how to stop it. Too late, she realized there had been other water she could have pulled from. A body of water much smaller than the broad river: the waterfall in the oasis. But she'd not thought of that, only the bottomless, endless river and so now the deluge had begun.

It had already started to sweep past her calves and even as it ran, she felt the strength of the current and knew it was rising fast. All too soon it was to her knees and she saw the leg of one of the leathered crones, the one she and Barruch had freed, go floating past. As far as she could see in each direction, the rain beat against the surface of the shallow lake that used to be a plain. Everywhere she looked.

Barruch.

She stole a frantic and harried glance toward the oasis. It looked like an island from where Alaysha stood, fighting the current. She'd never make it to him in time. She knew he could swim, all horses could, but if the oasis got swallowed by the ever-growing lake, he'd never be able to swim far enough to save himself.

And neither would she.

A sob broke through her throat. She couldn't tell if she was crying because her face was streaming with the water the heavens were unleashing. She forced her legs to move against the weight of water and current. To get to Barruch, she had to go parallel to the movement of water. Perhaps if she could get to him, then they could ride the current to dry land. The water would have to meet an end sometime. Somewhere.

The thought made her think of the river she'd imagined. They said it had no end. No bottom.

If she'd psyched the water from there and brought it here, it was very likely there would be no end.

She could barely see even if she squinted into the rain, and the only thought that would come to her was that she couldn't even psych the land dry again because the water would just collect in clouds above her and ultimately let go when they grew too heavy.

The only other thought that came after that, before she started paddling desperately toward the oasis, was that she'd rather lose control than risk bringing such devastation again.

One hundred mount strides to the oasis. She'd counted them that first day. How many arm strokes in water would that be? She was already waist deep, the water roaring in her ears. She thought in the distance she could see a blur of black. She struggled to hear anything besides water slicing into water. No sounds of whinnied protest or fear met her ears, but she knew it was Barruch. She knew he would come for her. To be with her.

She forged on. It was him. She knew it. He was coming closer, but he was struggling, she could tell. Off course and working hard to stay in line, the current was doing its best to bring him where it wanted. Forward. To the north. Away from her.

She shouted at him but she didn't think her throat was even able to make a sound. She certainly couldn't hear her voice in the fierceness of the storm. She watched, helpless, as he went under, came up again, and then began to move so quickly north with the current that she knew he'd filled his belly with fruit.

It was possible his stomach was twisted.

It was very possible the pain would keep him from being able to swim.

It was possible he'd lost his energy.

And it was very possible he was going to die.

CHAPTER 19

She thought she heard a shout, but she knew she'd been too paralyzed to open her mouth. She was treading water, sobbing soundlessly and watching him stream away.

Then another shout sounded and ripples appeared in the water, large circular waves that made her think foolishly that a mountainous finger had dipped itself into the lake. The oasis shivered like a heat wave and then, between her and Barruch, a movement.

Her mount seemed to be gliding backwards against the current; Alaysha found herself standing again. Her toes reached into the mud, feeling small cracks that reminded her of the veins across Theron's nose.

Then she wasn't fighting the current anymore. The water everywhere began to ease up.

She imagined she'd somehow managed to stem the power, stop it in some way. Her fear for Barruch, her worry at causing worse devastation than draining. The elation of it filled her chest and spilled out in laughter as she saw Barruch stop moving altogether. He found his legs.

And it seemed the water was obeying her.

She felt like a goddess in the moment. She believed she was capable of anything.

And then she saw the cracks in the earth where the water was draining away. A score of crevices so many she couldn't count them, and at least a dozen chasms so wide a man could lie in them and still have headroom.

The Earth had split itself apart to save her and her trusted beast. And she knew the power had not come from her spirit. The land around her was a sodden mess of new muck and fissures filled with water. The rain was still heaving itself downward, and it seemed the cracks were deepening to accommodate the volume. Her only hope until the power waned was to get Barruch to the mound of Earth that once was the oasis. If the rain kept coming she wasn't sure even if it would be able to withstand the torrent no matter how deep the cracks went. They would have to fill some time.

She tried to whistle for Barruch, but found doing so in the rain more difficult than she'd expected. She settled for shouting and waving her arms. She hoped he could find a way through the muck.

When he finally swung his long neck in her direction, she thought it moved a little too slowly. Fatigue beyond measure, she realized. The oasis for now was out of the question.

She had to work each step to pull her feet through the muck and against the sucking draw of each step forward. Focusing on the movement, she was able to ignore the way the rain felt striking her skin. Twice she reached fissures too wide to step over and had to put all her strength into jumping across them. The closer she got to Barruch, the wider they grew.

When she finally made it near enough to her beloved mount, she could tell how exhausted he was. He stood on the opposite side of a chasm wide enough she'd have to swim it to reach him. Alaysha noticed far fewer crevices on his side. For some reason, this wide channel had opened near enough to him that it drained the water without need of further splits.

She was grateful, but thoroughly confused.

"We are lucky, old man," she shouted to him and felt relief rush over her when he neighed in return.

"I'm coming."

She plunged into the newly rent and swollen river and swam, hand over her shoulder for several minutes before climbing with effort onto the other side. She couldn't stand straight away; her legs and arms were trembling from exhaustion. All she could do was stretch her hand forward on the ground so she could touch his hoof. She could have wept when she felt his nose against her fingers.

"I couldn't leave you, could I?" Alaysha felt her eyelids close from tiredness, not the need to block out the rain.

In fact, if she thought about it, the raindrops did seem less intense.

"I think the rain is stopping."

Barruch blew air on her arm and she could swear it was the last thing she felt before her face grew warm and her eyelids bright enough she had to shield them.

She'd fallen asleep, obviously. The sun had found its way through the mist of old humidity left over from the torrent. She rolled over, still sore, but grateful. The ground was oily from the wet surface and she could see, as she sat up, that muck covered her from head to toe.

She sent a thoughtful glance to the river next to her, but shrugged. She'd just get filthy again. Maybe she'd wait the night at the oasis and head back to Sarum with the new sun. Her stomach growled irritably.

"Did you save me any food, old man?"

Barruch stomped. She was pleased to see he'd recovered enough to do so. "You must have had a good nap, too. Shall we?"

She stood shakily, but decided against lifting herself to his back. Instead, she reached for his lead and sent her feet in the direction of the oasis. He came with her almost reluctantly.

"I know. I can think of no better place than our little cavern or Saxa's cottage or Yuri's stables where you have so many fillies you enjoy, but it will have to be the open stars tonight."

They would get a decent rest, some honey, and maybe a few eggs if the rain hadn't washed the oasis clean of food. A quick wash in the waterfall, and then sleep through the night.

She doubted anything would wake her.

Twice through the night she woke to the sense that someone was watching her. Each time she grumbled to Barruch in the dark to go to sleep. When she woke with the sounds of birds filtering their song through the branches, she doubted her trusty mount would have been so sentimental as to watch her sleep, but she couldn't find anyone lurking close enough to warrant the belief that someone else had been there.

"Leftover magics," she decided aloud. The crones had wrapped this place in spells to keep Yenic safe even as they sacrificed themselves to Alaysha's power.

The thought made her freeze midstride. Three powerful women letting themselves be murdered, knowing their lines would disappear with them made no sense. As it turned out, Yenic's mother had been secreted far enough away that she could continue the line and so the sacrifice of the fire crone was successful. The babe who controlled the air was smuggled too, no one knew where; that made the elder of air's sacrifice assured if not totally impractical. It made sense that the elders had made provisions, yes, but it didn't make sense that they would only protect two of the three.

Three witches dead at her hand. Three left alive. Wind, water, fire. But where was earth? Without the fourth there could be no balance, and she stared at the cracks in the soil, the fissures now turned to brooks, the chasms turned to rivers.

She recognized the power now as surely as she recognized her own hand.

The witch who commanded the clay was alive.

CHAPTER 20

Aedus met her at the gate looking breathless with excitement. Even from a dozen mount strides away, Alaysha could make out the glow of exertion on her face beneath the strings of muddy hair. She shifted one foot to the next impatiently and grabbed Alaysha's leg when Barruch reined in close enough.

The girl wasted no time delivering her news.

"I know where he is. I know where Edulph is."

Alaysha's gaze went to the gates with a feeling of certain dread. "Inside?"

Aedus nodded. "Inside but not where you think. Inside the mountain." She took in Alaysha from head to toe. "What happened?"

"I'm not sure," she said. "Something—something very strange."

"Here too," Aedus said.

"How so?"

"You'll see."

The girl looked incredibly old in the moment. If it weren't for the strings of matted hair, the bare feet, and the filthy face, Alaysha would swear she looked at a woman grown.

"Tell me," she said.

"I'll do better." Aedus grinned broadly. "I'll take you."

Alaysha expected the girl to go back to the gates, but she pushed through a thicket of shrubs in the same direction as her nohma's cottage. She climbed down from Barruch's saddle and gripped his lead.

"How far?"

"You'll be amazed." Aedus said from over her shoulder. "I watched Yenic like you told me to and soon enough after a couple of days I noticed he left the city to come out here. Always with a trencher of bread, sometimes a cauldron of broth."

"Food for someone."

"Food for Edulph."

"You're sure you saw him."

The girl stepped over a log that had fallen onto the path. By daylight, Alaysha found herself seeing the old terrain with six-year-old eyes. She could have led Aedus directly to the cottage but when Aedus veered right and headed back toward the city, Alaysha got confused.

"I thought it was at the hovel."

She saw the girl shook her head.

"Better than that." She peered over her shoulder again. "Maybe you should leave him back there." She nodded toward the ruins of the cottage. "It gets a little snaky."

Alaysha considered going back, but now she was so close she hated to do so. She took Barruch's lead and wrapped it around a tree.

"We won't be long," she told him, then faced Aedus. "Let's get going."

The girl continued on, ducking beneath low hanging branches and continuing the chatter as she went.

"When I remember that night you were with him, I couldn't recall seeing him coming through the way we'd both come." She halted suddenly, cocking her head as though she'd heard something but after a few moments spoke again. "I came out to the ruins and looked around and noticed a subtle path that led away from the cottage but toward the mountains. I knew it wasn't deer. The ground didn't tell that tale."

"It was too recent."

"No. Too old."

Alaysha gave her a queer look and then studied the ground. "It looks like it was once a well-worn path."

"Right. So I watched Yenic one morning, stuffing bread into his tunic. He came out here."

A thought began to dawn on Alaysha, one that made her feel queasy.

"He didn't follow me that night; he was coming back from Edulph."

Aedus gave the briefest of compassionate nods. "I'm sorry, Alaysha."

She tried to shrug it off and appear as though it didn't bother her, but she couldn't help feeling a grimace had frozen on her face. She had to say something to get rid of it.

"Did you go in?"

Aedus looked at the ground. "No."

Alaysha guessed she'd not wanted to see the brother who had betrayed her. Not by herself.

"You want me to go?"

She looked like she took a deep breath, bracing herself. "I'll go with you."

"Are you sure?"

It took a moment, but the girl nodded. "I'm ready."

Alaysha went first, entering the mouth of the cave, a cave very much like the one she'd holed up in herself after her nohma died. It was of a height that made walking upright easy, almost as though it was a dug tunnel. Every so many feet for a long while, there was a natural skylight varying in size from that of a fist to a head for any available light to get through. The farther in they went, she noticed corroded discs that were convex in shape. She wasn't sure at first what they were until she spied an old oil lamp next to one of them.

"Whoever used this tunnel found a way to use these to bring the light," she murmured.

"What?"

Aedus stepped close and Alaysha scraped at the surface to show her. "See? Polished copper beneath." She looked back and could clearly make out a line of discs that in their day would have reflected one to the next. Strangely, though, they pointed in the wrong direction to be bringing light into the tunnel from the outside. It was peculiar, but it had to be used to help light move.

"Why not torches?" Aedus held hers up and it sputtered. Alaysha peered farther down the tunnel.

"It goes for a long way. Maybe they were worried about losing the air."

In fact, the more she looked, the more directions she could see the tunnel branching off into.

"We're going to get lost," Alaysha said. "I should have brought something to mark as we go."

Aedus peered into the darkness. "If Yenic can find his way, we can." She ran the torch across the floor of the cave, then along the walls. "All we have to do is follow the sconces and the discs. I bet if Yenic has Edulph in here somewhere, he would need some markings to get around. And I bet he used what was here."

Alaysha shot her a proud smile. "Good thinking."

The girl shrugged. "Common sense."

As they moved along, and the tunnel got more humid, Alaysha sensed they were heading toward the center of the mountain. It grew so hot she felt the sweat run down her spine, and just as she was about to give the escapade up for ridiculous, the tunnel broke into a room twice as wide as the bathhouse.

That was where the similarity ended.

Inside, the chamber caught the light of their torch and reflected it repeatedly by itself, lighting the room as though it had an open roof to the sun. The walls were smooth and polished and as white as any tooth on Bodicca's arm bracelet.

"Dear deities, it looks like the inside of the skull." She said as she stepped in. She expected Aedus to say something and when she didn't, Alaysha turned to her.

The girl stood there paralyzed. Her face held shock and recognition, and a queer seesawing of her jaw had begun making the girl's teeth grind. She began to tremble, her scrawny shoulders moving as though someone was shaking her.

"What is it, Aedus?"

"I don't know."

"It's beautiful." Alaysha could hear the wonder in her own voice and reached out to touch the wall. It felt cool, but warmed to her Palm almost as though a vibration hummed through it.

"Yes," Aedus said. "But something else too." She looked to be working at pulling in air and Alaysha put her arms around the girl's shoulders, hugging her close until the trembling stopped.

"I'm sorry," the girl said and Alaysha smiled for her, was about to tell her everything was fine when a feeble shout met her ears and she turned to the center, where she thought it had come from.

"Edulph?" She heard herself saying, but no other sound came back. She nodded toward the dais in the middle, a granite block out of place in the cavern, then she looked at Aedus. "Sounded like it came from there."

She had to pull Aedus along as she rushed over and climbed the smooth steps of the dais to peer down. What looked rectangular from the door appeared circular from on top of the platform.

And it was hollow.

With a quick breath, Aedus leaned over, holding the torch aloft. Below, about a kubit down, sat Edulph. His moustache and hair looked singed and the hands he held in front of his face to block the sudden light were scarred and blistered.

Alaysha felt no pity for the man, but she reminded herself that this was Aedus's brother. It must be painful for her nonetheless.

Aedus was the one who spit into the hole. "You're a disgrace to our people, Edulph," she said. "You're a shame to us."

The sly grin, despite the obvious pain and hunger, stole over his face when he recognized his young sister.

"Aedus," he said, his voice crackling from lack of use. "Get me out of here."

"You should rot here."

"I am rotting, can't you see?" He held up his hands to the light. "Throw down a rope."

"There is no rope."

"Go get some before she gets back."

Alaysha pushed Aedus aside. "Who? Before who gets back?" She knew the answer even if he refused to give it.

"You're as bad as she is, wanting answers, always answers." He began mumbling incoherently, punctuating his words with a few vehement strikes to his face.

"I won't say anything. To speak is to die." He began to sob.

Alaysha felt something niggle up her spine. "I won't kill you."

"The answer will kill me."

Alaysha scanned Aedus's face, hoping she could interpret her brother's dementia.

"Edulph, brother, who has you so frightened?"

Alaysha wanted to hear the name even if she knew whose it would be. She waited, breath inhaled as she peered down, watching Edulph rocking back and forth, holding his hands to his chest like a hurt child.

"Who?" She pressed.

When she expected the answer, a voice crept to her from behind that made the fine hairs on the back for neck perk to attention. She knew when she turned around who would be standing there.

"I asked why you're here, Alaysha?"

She pushed herself to stand and turned slowly to face Yenic, praying he didn't have a weapon in his hand. She raised her hands in surrender as she faced him.

Relief swept over her when she saw the only thing he held onto was a bucket and a length of rope.

"I might ask you the same thing." She took a step toward him, indicating with her palm that Aedus should stay still.

Yenic looked down at his load. "I've come to feed him."

Aedus jumped to her feet even as Edulph began squealing in the pit like a pig for its dinner. "You've had him all this time." Her voice trembled with accusation and hurt.

Yenic nodded. "Of course. You don't think I'd hand him over to the conqueror until we were sure of his intent." He looked at Alaysha. "Alaysha? Surely you can see that?"

She wanted to believe him. It could be true. She licked her lips, wanting to tell him she understood. "Why didn't you tell me?"

He had no time to answer. Even as his mouth opened, the tunnel emptied a dozen or more men into the room and it erupted with activity. At least three dozen of Yuri's guard stormed the cavern, spreading out in battle positions, several jumping toward Yenic before he could drop the bucket.

It was the first time she'd seen him in action except for the one-on-one with Gael. This time, Yenic's movements were fluid and somewhat magical. He ducked and dodged, using the contents of the bucket — hot soup, apparently — as the first weapon.

He was doing just fine until Yuri strode into the cavern, Bodicca alongside him. With a short nod, he set the fierce woman on Yenic, and despite his obvious non-compunction to do battle with a woman, she showed her obvious mastery within heartbeats.

Alaysha had never seen such a method of fighting before. All over the ground, wrapping herself over him, sneaking under him, grabbing for his neck even as he worked to keep her off her feet, Bodicca showed no mercy and seemed to need none. In the end, it was Yenic who lay on the floor of the cave, Bodicca over him, her forearm across his neck, the Python thickness of her legs wrapped around his, his chest pinned beneath her hips.

The others came to her aid and extracted him from her tight grip within moments, pulling his arms behind his back, then bending him forward to wrap a heavy chain around his neck.

In all the time, Yuri said nothing. Now he moved to the center of the cave and addressed Yenic with something of a victorious air. "It appears as though you have killed my trainer. That's an offense to me that is punishable by death." He sent a scathing glance toward Alaysha, giving her an opportunity for argument, but sending the message that he expected none. She thought he wanted to chastise her but opted against it.

"Even worse," Yuri said. "Is to know you have been harboring a man who threatened to annihilate my entire city and those who live in its borders." He looked toward the dais where Edulph's shouts still sounded. "Do not feed him; he doesn't deserve to eat," he said to a few of his soldiers. "And remain here until I decide what to do with him."

He glared at Alaysha. "You will leave, Witch, and return to your hovel until I have need of you." He turned and went back out of the tunnel, all but a dozen of his men following him. The remainder took stations around the dais.

Alaysha looked to Aedus whose shoulders had slumped miserably. She reached her hand out to the girl and they trudged from the tunnels quietly, sullen. The only thing that brightened Aedus's spirit was the sight of several small beetles scuttling from beneath a rock she kicked when they exited the tunnel and into the woods around Alaysha's cave.

"What of Yenic?" Aedus asked.

"What do you think?"

"I think you're going to try to free him."

Alyasha didn't need to provide an answer.

CHAPTER 21

Yenic looked tired and haggard by the time she made it to the courtyard, where she knew by the gathered crowd that Yuri had decided to dispense justice.

It was obvious that the battle between him and Bodicca hadn't ended in the cave; Yenic's face was bleeding below the cheek and Bodicca stood beside him, holding the other end of the chain that was wrapped around his neck. She had come through battle with a swollen and purple eye. Her nose was a squashed flat piece of broken cartilage.

It pleased Alaysha to see that he hadn't gone down without a fight. She felt proud of him for a brief moment, then anxiety clamped down around her when she saw Aislin step forward from the throng, pulling along the girl from the parapet room, her face still swathed in linens.

"My child for yours," she shouted.

It took Yuri a moment to respond and even from where Alaysha stood, she could see that his mind was working, even if his face gave away nothing. Finally, he rattled Yenic's chain and shouted so loud the entire crowd would be able to hear.

"Do you think I would give up a killer to save a witch? You offer me nothing."

Alaysha's heart sank, even if she knew he was merely strategizing.

Her father's face, normally pale and solemn began to redden despite the obvious working to keep his composure. She almost felt sorry for him.

"Where is my son?"

Yenic shuffled his feet and Alaysha's eyes went to Aislin's, whose expression turned to something nasty looking. In the moment, she believed the witch would set Yuri to flame and she wondered at Yuri's courage to stand against her.

"That's a dangerous accusation to make against a woman who can wipe you out within a heartbeat," Aislin shouted.

Yuri's stance never shifted. "You have Saxon. I know this."

Aislin lifted the doppelgänger's arm to the air. "I seem to have your witch as well."

The crowd shouted out orders to kill, and even though Alaysha knew Aislin was merely trying to outsmart Yuri, she still felt the snake of anxiety tingle up her spine. She watched Yuri's face with interest.

"I want my son and I'm not inclined to show mercy if I don't find him."

He motioned to Bodicca, who pulled the sword from her back and took a swinging stance, ready to divest Yenic of his head. Alaysha wanted to shout out to him, but the words choked off in her throat as Aislin pulled the linen from the doppelgänger's face.

The crowd within view of the girl whooped their pleasure, some of them yelled at Aislin to be done with it and kill the witch. Alaysha thought her legs went to water. But for the fact that the girl's chin was a mess of blackened skin and blistering sores, she could have been her true double. She sent a fleeting glance to Yuri, who remained impassive. Yenic, however, had buckled beneath the sight. He was trying to maintain his feet under the weight of the chains.

Aislin stepped closer to Yuri, pulling the doppelgänger with her and twisted sideways to address the crowd. "My son, your son. We both want something from the other but neither of these is the true price."

She dropped the girl's hand, and for some reason, the girl's eyes moved across the crowds and found Alaysha's. Their gazes held, and her memory reeled backward so far her ears were filled with piteous squalls of a hungry infant. She felt again the warmth of another body next to hers for brief moments, realized the sense of a tiny hand grasping her heel.

Her sister. Her baby sister.

Alaysha wanted to cry out, and saw her own hand lifting to the air, reaching out to her. How had she let that memory go to, that memory so full of contentment and peace it would have been pleasurable in the dark nights in the caverns to remember it. Alaysha took an involuntary step forward, thinking to rush the space and grasp at her sister, but something was wrong with the girl's face. It was crumpling. Fire leapt from her tunic and danced up her arm. She shrieked with such pain, Alaysha swore she could feel it in her own chest, burning, such searing agony. In heartbeats, the girl was gone, and all that was left was a smoldering pile of cinders.

After that, nothing made sense. Alaysha noted bursts of fire leaping through the crowd, people screaming, scattering. She thought she saw Yenic collapse to his knees; Yuri's guards stormed the fire witch only to catch flame before they took five steps.

More fires began to hopscotch through the remaining crowd, dancing from one head to the next. Flames leapt from a man's tunic and danced up his arm.

All of this she saw but could not process. She watched Yuri draw his blade and push Bodicca out of the way, as he hefted his own blade towards Yenic's neck.

Aislin's cold smile was the only thing that did register.

Alaysha had wanted Yuri dead, but in the moment that he froze beneath Aislin's power, in the heartbeat when she swore she reached out to his heart, it had begun to grow feverish with blood. She thought she felt regret there, grief as well, as she reached out to him, drew her psyche to his sweat and pores and the liquid in his body. She thought of the broad river so deep it had no bottom, so wide it had no banks, and she thought how cold it must be there.

Then she thought how absolutely she hated Aislin. She had the vague sense that it was raining, that the courtyard had emptied of people, that both Yuri and Aislin were watching her with some odd expectation, and then they just fell, both of them, where they stood. Alaysha felt a prickly tension in her neck. Her hand went to it, not thinking, and came away purple and sticky.

She thought she was falling and thought it odd that falling could feel so much like being scooped up and carried.

CHAPTER 22

She woke to the sound of dripping water. It seemed as though the bed she was lying on was made of stone. The air held so much dampness she could have believed she was sleeping beneath the broad sea except she could still breathe. Each inhale smelled like she was dragging in a dog's breath, but still, she could breathe.

She rolled over to her side and groaned. A scuffling sound came from behind her and she tried to jump to her feet, ready to face whatever sweating beast was fouling the air. She didn't make it to her knees before she teetered back over.

"You're awake." A voice came from the shadows, and she felt around in front of her wondering why she couldn't see, then realized she was facing a wall.

"I am," she said, trying to figure out why she was so disoriented and why the words had such a hard time moving across a tongue that was as thick as it was. Her ears too must have grown excess flesh; she could swear she heard Gael's voice answering.

She twisted onto her bottom so she could see where she was. There was no panic. That must mean something. A pool of light played with the shadows on the floor. She realized the shadows were tree branches.

She knew where she was.

Her little cave in the woods. She was home. That must mean these blurry creatures shuffling about in the half dark were Aedus and — dare she believe it — Gael.

"How long?" she asked, knowing as she did the skylight told her early evening. The moon loved to dance over that hole. It was why she'd chosen this cave.

"A couple of hours." Aedus's voice.

Alaysha leaned back and closed her eyes, trying to create some sense in all that had happened. When she opened them, Gael's furrowed brow had somehow crept close to hers. She reached out to run a finger across it. She thought she saw him ease his eyelids closed, but she couldn't tell in the light.

"It is you," she said.

"Yes," he said. "Did you sleep well?"

She smiled, thinking about the time she'd asked him the same question. "At least I don't snore."

"The Deities you don't."

Alaysha tried to stand and felt Gael's hand on her back. "Careful," he said. "You'll be dizzy."

"Can you walk?" Aedus's voice again. She stepped into the pool of light where Alaysha could see her.

"Of course." Alaysha took a step and wondered why so many stars had suddenly come out. She heard Gael chiding Aedus.

"Why did you have to shoot her anyway?"

"I told you; I shot them all. I had to."

He grunted and hefted Alaysha into his arms. She felt safe, comfortable, and thoroughly miserable. Her complaints sounded weak even to her own ears.

"We have to get moving," Aedus explained. "If you're coming around, so are they, and we don't want them — either of them — finding us here."

By them, Alaysha assumed she meant Yuri and Aislin. For some reason she had the feeling she should remember something and then it flooded into her consciousness.

"They have Yenic."

"Bodicca has Yenic," Aedus corrected her.

"What was going on, Aedus?"

The girl shrugged. "I don't know, but none of it looked promising."

The steady rise and fall of Gael's chest was nearly as mesmerizing as a lullaby; Alaysha had to work to keep her eyes open and her mind focused. She let her head fall into the crook of his elbow.

"Something isn't right."

"You're finally talking sense," Aedus said, and Gael murmured his agreement.

"It didn't look like anyone was going to be living through that."

Alaysha realized somehow he'd been there. She didn't care how or why. As events began flooding back, she was just relieved they'd both been there. A few heartbeats more and she wasn't sure what would've happened. Just recalling the sense of controlled, but very fierce power slithering from her in tendrils of incredible emotion made her realize how much the energy could take and give. How powerful it really was. It unnerved her.

"The city—"

"Is wet, but not flooded. I must have got you out in time." Gael gave her a squeeze as Aedus said it, almost as though he was grateful.

"You were there," Alaysha whispered.

"At the last, yes."

Aedus seemed to grow impatient. "We have to move. We're not safe here."

Thinking made Alaysha's head hurt, but she knew the safest bet was within the tunnels. "There's a tunnel over there. It goes for long time. I've never reached the end but I've never run out of air either." As a suggestion, it was weak and she knew it, but she also figured no one would be interested in following a tunnel very far.

"I can walk," she told Gael, but he ignored her and forged ahead. In truth, she was still terribly tired, and she welcomed the chance to close her eyes. It was testament to Gael's robust strength that he had been able to shake off Aedus's sleep darts before so easily. It made her wonder what effect they would leave on Yenic or Yuri or Aislin. Yuri and Aislin. They'd wanted each other dead, but there was something more in the undercurrents of that exchange. She just couldn't fight her way through the grief or betrayal to decipher it. She wasn't sure which emotion she should feel, and decided neither was the best choice. At least for the time being.

She must have dozed, because her mind stopped working and instead she dreamed of her seeds. She came to consciousness telling herself she wouldn't forget to collect them, then realized they were no longer walking. Instead of being cushioned in Gael's arms, she was lying between him and Aedus in the deep dark. A draft of air stole its way from the bowels of the tunnel, raising the hair on her arms. Aedus was snoring. Gael was not.

"Feeling better?" he asked, his lips close to her ear.

She nodded. "How did you know I was awake?" She realized his palm was on her belly as she asked it.

"I could feel the shift in your breathing."

She reached to touch his fingers with her own, and thought better of it. The last thing she wanted to do was hurt him any more. She was finally beginning to understand the pain of loss and love and it was too much to stand against; she couldn't offer him false hope knowing he'd grieve later.

"Gael," she started to say but his palm moved to cup her chin.

"I hated this tattau before," he murmured. "Now it haunts me."

She reached to take his hand from her face gently. "Please," she said, not sure what she meant by it, but hoping he'd understand her hesitation.

"I'm fine," he said. "We've made our choices, and I understand them."

"You don't sound fine."

The only sound for a short time was Aedus's soft snoring, but when he did speak it was with a voice thick with emotion. "It's only because I still ache for you. I worry for you."

Two very different emotions, and yet Alaysha understood them both. The worry, the lust, the sense that both could become so tangled together. She thought of Yenic and felt a stab of regret, then of longing. Still, knowing he was so completely his mother's tool, she loved him.

She knew she would be lying to herself if she didn't admit to feeling a similar want for Gael. There was something primal about having another person want you so badly they would offer their body in protection for your own, about another's willingness to take even a shadow of you if you would offer it. It was a different need than the one she felt for Yenic, but it was no less strong. She reached for his hand in the dark and held it. The flesh of his palm was hot and callused, so much so that she couldn't stop imagining how it would feel smoothing out her skin, catching against the fine hairs of her body.

She might know she wanted him as much as he did her, but she also knew it wasn't companioned by love. Only desire.

His voice was in her hair, the heat of his breath tickling her earlobe. "The air is cooler down the tunnel," he whispered.

"I can't do that to you," she murmured and felt his arm wrap over her stomach.

"I can live without you if I can have just one memory to fill the loneliness."

His hand slipped beneath her tunic and brushed against her thigh. His touch was so light, she doubted he felt anything against the hardness of his callused skin, but when his breathing grew shorter and he cupped her from behind, pulling her against him, she knew he didn't need to feel her skin to know her response.

She felt his lips on her eyelids, small fluttering kisses as silent as the darkness, then brushing against her cheek, seeking her mouth until she parted for him and tasted his tongue.

She thought again, briefly, of Yenic, poor Yenic, and wondered where he was, then felt such shame she didn't dare breathe until the grief of it all would just go away.

Gael's arms encircled her and then she was airborne, lifted against his chest so effortlessly she could be flying of her own accord as he stood. His mouth went to her neck, then nipped against her ear.

"It's a kindness you're showing me, Alaysha. No more. Let me be yours just this once and I'll be yours until my death."

She wanted him; they both knew it, and she would be a fool to pretend she wasn't responding, but it was selfish. Too selfish. "It's not fair to you."

His response to her protest was to claim her mouth, devouring every inch of it, teasing her tongue. She was weightless in his arms; he dropped her legs so that she hung against him, not touching the ground, feeling every measure of him against her. She realized her arms had wound past his neck and her fingers were in his hair, that he had somehow managed to pull her legs around his waist and was holding them there captive. That his heart was beating against her own in a terrified, primal staccato.

She realized they were moving, that he was striding with her through the cooler air of the tunnel with such ease he could have carried no burden at all, and when they had gone far enough out of Aedus's earshot, only then did he speak again, pulling his lips from hers and burying them in her neck.

"I would never force you. You decide what's best for you, but know if I have you no more than this one night it will be enough for me."

If she could have found a way to speak through the tightness in her throat, she might have protested. She might have reminded herself she was bound to the youth who thought her dead, but then she remembered the grief of why he thought it so and all she could do was search for Gael's mouth with hers to stop herself from recalling the pain.

He gasped like a man finding air after a long spell underwater. She thought she heard him moan but she couldn't be sure. He seemed almost afraid she'd change her mind as he let her to her feet; his hands roamed her skin in every place it was free of linen or hide, and when they weren't on her, they were peeling at his own leathers.

He reached for her hand and used it to trace the pattern of scars on his chest. His voice came to her in a hoarse whisper. "I'd take all of these and more for you," he said. "Know that."

She could only nod before his mouth was on hers again, his tongue invading her in ways she was too ignorant to respond to. She let him explore where he would without resistance. He guided her to his pile of leathers and tunics where he methodically peeled away her clothes and added them to the impromptu bed. If it was cool in the tunnel, she'd never know it; his body was warm and his breath a hot draft that touched the hairs on her skin and left them laying low in submission.

He at once began to take his time with her, letting his breath touch her skin before his lips, his tongue, sometimes his hands. She knew each time he put a callous to her flesh that it felt sacred to him, somehow, that his kisses and the way he tasted her skin might have been his opportunity to imbibe finally from a forbidden wine. She felt like a fine libation in his hands; she felt like the fleshly altar of a goddess.

More than that, he made her feel as though his heated roaming of her skin wasn't enough, that she had to touch him in return. She found she wanted to trace each scar to its origin and feel the veins throb beneath his skin.

Once, he put his ear to her heart and let it lie there for several heartbeats. He put her hand on his. When he was satisfied of something only he understood, he reached to kiss her, long and torturously slow, with a thoroughness that made her arch against him in need. She had to let go a pleading moan before he took her, finally, with a masterful but tender plunge.

His gasp sounded like a prayer.

CHAPTER 23

When she woke next, she was beside Aedus again, but she didn't feel Gael next to her. She groped for him in the darkness, afraid suddenly that something might have happened to him. She bolted up only to see a light sputtering its way toward her in the tunnel, a large shadow hulking along with it. When it edged around the curve, she saw Gael's face in the light it cast. She had never seen him as peaceful, and she felt a flush overtake her face and neck.

"Where did you go?" she asked him as he settled down next to her, his great muscled thigh touching her own.

"To see how far the tunnel goes."

"You should've slept, reserved your strength."

"I didn't want to sleep."

"You should get some rest."

He reached across her to shake Aedus, who still snored lightly. She felt a tension at his touch, as though he was restraining himself, but he said nothing about the night they'd spent. "There's a room, not bigger, but more air. Lots of old oil lamps."

"Very far?"

Aedus moaned and rolled away, leaving Alaysha feeling chilly on that side.

Gael pushed himself to a stand and bent to pick Aedus up.

"Leave me be," the girl grumbled. "I dreamed of cats growling all night and barely slept a wink."

Gael chuckled. "You'll have a better pillow against my chest. Calm, little one. You know we have to keep moving."

"Some pillow," she said. "Just as hard as the stone floor."

"But far warmer," he told her, and she mumbled her agreement.

Alaysha fell into step with him, holding onto the torch so they could both see. "What do you think will happen, Gael?" She asked.

"I think whoever woke first will have put the other to torture."

Alaysha thought about that. If Yuri came to first, she knew the one place he would think of that could contain a witch without concern for his own welfare. If Aislin awoke first, she'd undoubtedly bring Yuri to the same place: a cavern filled with all sorts of torture devices.

"The bathhouse," she murmured, and Gael grunted.

"Neither will give up the other," he said. "The Emir will die trying to get his son back."

It hurt, that short, truthful statement, but it also made her wonder how far Aislin would go to save Yenic. She thought there might still be hope for him.

"I don't understand what's going on," she admitted.

"Your father has lost Sarum."

"I don't care about that."

"You should. Do you think the witch lets him live because she's afraid of him?"

"Lets him live?"

Gael turned to look over his shoulder at her. His face looked haunted in the play of torchlight. "For a warrior you are young in the ways of war."

"Then explain it."

"If she wanted the city, she could just take it. If she wanted him dead, she would've killed him. She wants something else. Something he has that she doesn't."

"What could that be?"

She saw his shoulders move in a shrug. "Information."

"But what could he know?"

By now they had reached the room. It was small and cramped, filled with spent oil lamps and dusty amphorae stacked against one wall and tumbling into a crevice farther into the dark. It was far drier in this tiny room that she could have believed possible. It astounded her that a mountain she had lived in and so close to all these years could have so many secrets.

She touched one of the oil lamps, rubbing what looked like centuries of dust from the surface. "So what could he know, Gael?"

"What have you been doing these last few moons?"

"Besides being sick? Killing." The words stuck in her throat. She'd always hated using that word, truthful as it was.

"Killing who? Enemies? Warriors?"

The mud village had been a peaceful one. "No." She wanted to squirm. "Not the last one."

"No. Not the last."

"So what, what does he know?" She had the feeling she was missing something, something Gael wanted her to realize.

He smiled at her so smugly, she thought for a moment he would have made an excellent leader — if he knew the secret, he certainly hadn't made her think before now that he was privy to it.

"The witch of clay," she said, unable to stand the amazement in her own voice as she realized the truth.

Once Yuri had realized he'd managed to assassinate the elders, and that the other witches still lived, he'd obviously suspected what Alaysha had not, until she'd gone back to the village: that the elders had made a sacrifice of themselves to save the others. Aislin lived still. The air witch, though lost, had obviously been saved. Why not the witch of clay?

"But surely Aislin would know. Certainly, if Yenic was spared as she was, Aislin would know where her peers were." She didn't want to say that she thought she knew where this witch of clay might be.

"What if none of them knew? What if they didn't trust each other?"

"But they must have. They worked in harmony. They worked together to protect Yenic from me and from Yuri."

He gave her a steely look. "What if it wasn't Yuri they were protecting themselves from? What if their act was not one of defence, but of subtle assault?"

"That's ludicrous."

"His silver brow lifted. "Truly? Do not think, powerful as you are, that the three of them together couldn't stand against you?"

She thought about that, and the thought that her ego had been so great that she had never assumed anyone could stand against her, made her feel embarrassed. Gael adjusted Aedus in his arms, and took a few steps toward the wall where he eased himself down and against it. When he was sitting, Aedus in his lap, her head against his chest, he looked back at Alaysha.

"I think their plan was far grander than we believed. They're out to trap someone. Someone powerful. Or they have an agenda I can't decipher. But it involves Aislin. I know it does."

She shook her head, confused. "Why not the earth witch? Why couldn't it be her?"

He sighed heavily. "Because the earth witch is of my tribe."

It was such a bold statement, Alaysha thought she heard her jaw click open and hang there. She searched his face for signs of untruth and finding none, sat on a stone to mull it over.

"How close," she finally asked.

Again he shrugged. "Close enough I suppose that Saxon provides some protection."

"Protection for whom?"

"Haven't you guessed?"

She was tired of having to guess. She was tired of knowing nothing. She leaned forward, holding the torch high enough that she could see his face clearly. "How much do you know? Tell me everything."

"Precious little. Only those things Theron told me when I returned to the city."

"What does Theron have to do with this?"

"Apparently he's from my tribe." Gael sounded uncertain, confused, and angry that he had only just come into information that changed what he believed about himself for all this time. She could see him look down at Aedus and only then did his face soften.

He sighed heavily. "Theron has been leeching Saxon and adding the collected blood to drafts he's been giving to the Emir."

"You've known about this?"

"Yes. For a few fortnights. I assumed he believed the same as Saxa, that Yuri was ill and that he was doing his part in keeping him healthy."

"So you never questioned it."

He sent her a scornful look. "Have you ever questioned your father?"

She had to admit that questioning the Emir was out of the question for any warrior let alone his witch.

"But he could have been poisoning him."

Gael chuckled. "Only a fool would take his time murdering a man like Yuri. And Theron is no fool."

"What else did Theron tell you?"

"There wasn't much time to tell me anything. Just that you had to be saved above all else, even above Yuri or the witch—in spite of Yuri and the witch."

"And?"

"And that Saxa and I—our father was the youngest brother to the last witch."

"So if Yuri knows where she is, why is he not sending for her?"

"I never said he knew. I said only that Aislin believes he knows."

"And so far that is keeping him alive."

"That and the fact that Bodicca has Yenic."

"Fortunate for him," she said sourly.

"Fortunate indeed, for a man who knows so little. He believes he has control but he has been played by the forces around him. Much as we have been."

"Then what's this all about, Gael?"

"I don't know. I truly don't. But Theron seemed to believe that war is coming, and it will be a war the likes of which we've not yet seen. Subtle and covert, but it is coming."

"Edulph."

Gael nodded. "Edulph is mad, yes. But he speaks the same truth that Theron does."

She wanted to snort, but kept her depressive thoughts to herself. "Theron himself is mad."

"Theron is mad when the wind is Nor'south. He was taken in the first campaign; did you know that?"

She shook her head.

"Well, he was. While Saxa and I were born in Sarum, Theron has always been here. If he says war is coming, it's coming."

"Then I'd say we best get Edulph out of that pit before he decides to tell Aislin where the baby is."

CHAPTER 24

It would be easier if they knew what was truly going on, what her father and Aislin wanted, or even Edulph. One thing was for certain: Yuri and Edulph were mere men and could be controlled if necessary. The fire witch could not.

Alaysha so wanted to believe Yenic's mother was at the mercy of Yuri and not the other way around. It would be so much easier. She hated that the man who could show her only contempt and pain might be totally ignorant of the machinations going on about him.

Still. When it was all over, his ignorance would not spare him from her wrath.

They trod through the tunnels, hoping to come out somewhere that they'd recognize. The difficult thing then would be to re-enter the city, the Keep, and find the crystal room again in time to get Edulph out. While she thought they had been walking into the mountain, small alcoves broke open here and there to reveal light, and she realized that they were close to the outside. When they came upon a small cavern with ages of layers of bat guano, she knew they'd reached the end. They darted through a haze of wings and furry bodies furious and frightened at being disturbed.

The fresh air smelled divine.

"Where do you think we are?" she asked Gael as he prodded Aedus awake and set her on her feet in the early morning sunlight.

"My guess would be the southern forest at the back of the mountain."

It would've taken days to travel up or around the hulking stone from one end to the other, but somehow they gone clear through in a night.

"Does Yuri know about these tunnels?" she asked him.

"Some. It's why he didn't build on top. He didn't want to leave them open for attack."

"Or investigation."

Gael nodded. "There are many. Although I only thought there were the tunnels that opened from the Keep. If he'd known about all of them, he would have extended the city. You can bet on that." He seemed to be looking at her with fresh eyes. His own hair was coming unplaited, the brows that were usually smoke and silver mixed, were streaked with dirt. She remembered how he'd buried that unshaven and beautiful face into her neck and left a trail of masterful kisses down to her navel. When she recalled what happened next, she had to look away.

"Aedus, do you still have some of your sleeping potion?"

The girl fumbled into the pouch she had tied her waist. Out she pulled a small knife, stolen obviously, a dried apple, and a roll of leather. She passed the roll to Alaysha, who peeled it open.

"Quite ingenious," she said when she saw the hollowed out branch used as a blower and at least a dozen quills. All were translucent but one.

Aedus apologized. "The beetles aren't easy to find."

Alaysha glanced Gael's way. "Let's hope we can get in and out without too much hassle." She spent a few minutes looking over Aedus's hair and wondering if the girl's natural slinkiness could be of use enough to warrant letting her accompany them.

Aedus seemed to know what was going on behind Alaysha's crumpled brow.

"I'm coming," she said.

"I didn't say you weren't."

"You were thinking about it."

"Only because I want you safe."

"Safe means with you two."

Alaysha waited to see what Gael would say, and when he nodded, she let go a breath of anxiety. She didn't like the thought of re-entering Sarum, even through the tunnels: she had no idea whether Yuri or Aislin would be in control of them, and she wasn't sure which one she'd rather run into. Gael pulled the sword from its scabbard across his back and inspected the edge.

"If we encounter the witch," he said to Aedus. "You must dart her."

Aedus jiggled her head up and down.

"And if it's Yuri?" Alaysha asked as he studied her face.

"If it is the Emir, she will dart you."

Aedus started to protest, but Gael held up his hand. Alaysha knew he had seen her re-acquaintance with her sister.

"I need to know you won't open up the heavens on him, and so us."

Alaysha found her bare toes very interesting. "I won't. Not now."

"But another time."

She couldn't stop the nod. "I will kill him at some point."

He said nothing in argument; she was grateful. When he started away without comment, she followed him with a sigh, knowing the entrance they took would bring them to the crystal cavern.

"But you knew too, didn't you?" she asked him. "You knew my father has kept her all this time."

"I did."

She watched his back begin to disappear into the darkness ahead of her. "Why didn't you tell me, back at the well. Why didn't you say she was my sister?"

"And what would you have done?"

She didn't need to answer; he grunted then spoke over his shoulder. "I would not want to have known that pain for Saxa."

"So you kept it from me to spare me."

His shoulders moved in a short shrug. "There was nothing you could do."

"I could have killed him," she said, meaning her father.

"And so all of us," was his response before he stepped faster and went ahead enough she realized he didn't want to speak about it anymore.

The going was dark and wet. They fell into step together without thinking, and Alaysha found herself wondering what Gael's warrior training had been like, if he had suffered similar torments through Corrin as she had. Thinking about it made her recall the feel of his skin on hers and how the scars felt beneath her fingers as she traced them across his chest, over his shoulders, down his back. Her mind wandered to the feel of his hands on her skin and how delicious the calloused roughness of his palms felt. She wouldn't let herself think about what came next, but the memory at least eased her anxiety as they trudged through the dark.

She could tell when they drew near to the cavern because the air went to such a deathly quiet that something seemed to come beneath the air currents. She hadn't noticed it the first time, how it fairly vibrated with dignity. All thought dissipated like so much steam as she drew close. The hair on her arms stood to rapt attention and the back of her neck went cold.

"Do you feel it?" she asked aloud, not sure who she was speaking to, but certain someone else would understand. It was Aedus who answered, the small voice drifting from her elbow.

"It's the gods' place," she said and Alaysha felt herself nodding, unsure what that even meant.

"Gael?" Alaysha heard herself murmur.

"I'm here." His voice came from behind her; when she turned to it, she saw his broadsword held to the ready, what she could see of his face in the gloom and shadows of sputtering torchlight was guarded and pinched.

"Do you feel it?"

He nodded. "Death."

Indeed. One word spoke of all the energy she couldn't name, and whether it was a death past or a death to come didn't matter.

"Be ready," he said as he took deliberate steps to pass them, through the blackened maw of what proved to be the last round of turn. Beyond the darkness, Alaysha could make out the winking brightness of the smooth crystal within.

She realized that none of them had thought beyond reaching Edulph to actually wresting him from the clutches of the pit, and then it struck her that Gael had no intention of milking Edulph for information and then pulling him to safety.

He planned to extract the information and then kill him on the spot, leaving him useless to anyone afterwards. Assuming, of course, that Yuri's men hadn't already done so.

She turned to Aedus. "Perhaps you should wait here."

Gael made a sound that indicated he was not in agreement. "We need her. Come." He waggled the fingers of his left hand behind him and Aedus went forward obligingly.

"Sneak forward. See if he's still there. If he's alone."

The girl nodded. "I'll wave you in when it's clear."

Alaysha waited with lungs full of air. She wasn't sure what the chances were that the guard Yuri had left with Edulph was still in the cave. She hadn't seen them in the courtyard, but she'd been preoccupied then. Whatever the chances, Aedus would be in full view of danger, yet here the girl was, ready to accept such duty as though she was born to it.

"I don't like this." Alaysha protested. "She might not be safe."

Gael grunted. "She is safer than we are."

Safer? How could that be? The small form had entered the cavern and already seemed as large within it as an ant on forage. If someone was indeed inside...

Alaysha's breath let go in a noisy rush as she realized someone was lying in wait. Several men from all directions moved as one toward Aedus, and Alaysha's immediate thought to rush to her aid was thwarted by the hulking movement of a blur of black leather swooping through the entrance and swinging in one wide arc.

The head of the first man rolled toward Alaysha's feet and the insane thought that she recognized the face rattling through her mind got chased away by an instinct so ingrained she forgot who had trained her to it. She grabbed the head and launched it toward the second man who had dodged Gael's sword and was feinting forward to take out the mountain at his knees.

The mass struck the assailant's chest and Alaysha knew the fleeting emotion that crossed his face was one of revulsion. He didn't have time to shift expression; Gael lopped off his head and sent it flying sideways.

She had only the time to think Gael had been right all along when he'd said Aedus had never been in danger. It was true that Gael was making such short work of the ambushing guards, that he'd sent her in fully expecting to kill, knowing he would do so down to the last man.

She had a few moments to watch him swing, rest, step, swing again; until she thought what she was witnessing was less a battle and more an orchestrated training session. He seemed to sense where each opponent would be before his opponent did. A dozen of them came at him, and a dozen fell, each taking a chance of leaving their mark on him.

Some did, but even Alaysha could tell they were glancing blows at best.

She came to understand how his height became his greatest weapon.

Even as the last two fell, Alaysha could see Aedus running to the pit and realized Edulph was still inside, shouting at whoever was above him.

The last man to stand against the tide of Gael's swinging blood rush was a sole, hooded man who stood paralysed on his feet. His hands clasped something in front of his thighs. Gael halted, panting in front of him, his chest moving from effort. The men faced each other for several heartbeats before Alaysha realized that the man facing Gael was Theron and that the thing he held in front of him was Yuri's head.

CHAPTER 25

She wasn't certain how she ended up at Theron's feet, staring up into her father's lifeless eyes, a flood of tears captured in her own refusing to fall, but she was certain that Gael's hands were on her shoulders, pulling her away.

She tried to shrug them off.

"He was mine," was all she could say, whether she meant hers to kill or her father didn't matter.

"We have to get out of here," he told her, and Theron dropped the head into her hands.

"Take it," he said. "The witch needs it, yes, she does, more than the city does now."

Gael's hold grew insistent. "She's coming. We have to get Edulph out."

Alaysha stared down at the white hair turned pink from blood. "She can't harm us here. She hasn't the power." Even as she spoke, she remembered Aislin's quick hand streaking a macabre red grin across Corrin's throat.

Theron pushed at her. "The witch can't be seen with us when she comes, oh no, she can't. And she's coming. Oh yes, she is. With another dozen men."

Gael snorted derisively, and Theron touched him on the shoulder. "Men afraid of death have no other fear. The death you offer will be swift, but we know, oh yes, we do, that her deliverance will be one of agony. Spare them if you can."

"They're ours, then?"

Theron smiled humorously. "They were ours."

Alaysha wanted to rid herself of Yuri's head, and discovered it had made its way to entanglement within her fingers.

"Take it for us, witch," Theron said.

She couldn't look him in the eye. He looked so aggrieved. She sought out Aedus and noticed the girl had already unclothed several of the men of their tunics and had begun tying them together. Gael caught the direction of her glance and followed it with his own.

"Help get him out of there," he told her. "Then take Theron."

Without further word, he pushed Alaysha towards the pit, and with one last lingering look, captured her eyes with his. He said nothing more, just stepped behind Theron into the darkness of the middle tunnel.

She knew he would face Aislin and her men, and she knew he would meet each one with all the strength he could, until he could no more.

The clump in her throat would not go down no matter how much she swallowed and she had to work around it to speak, even if the words came out as nothing more than a whisper.

"Let's not waste the time he gives us," she said to no one, then grabbed the end of the tunic rope Aedus had begun stringing. She missed the end at first because she couldn't see through for the tears.

CHAPTER 26

The journey from the crystal cavern and to the tunnel seemed the longest of her life. It was a sober, silent track punctuated only periodically by Edulph's mad outbursts. Alaysha began to wonder if he had enough mind left to lead them to the wind witch when the time came.

Her heart ached. Her belly ached. Her eyes stung from unshed tears. She wondered, as they rushed through the semi dark, whether loving anyone was worth all the pain she felt. Gael. Her father. Nohma. Her mother and a sister she never knew. She felt for Aedus's hand in the gloom and when it fastened on the small fingers, everything seemed more pronounced. What was the point, even of living, when everything could end so quickly?

Time passed painfully slowly. Each time Edulph babbled about war coming on with blind speed, Alaysha had to stifle a shiver; Aedus squeezed her hand. Theron kept his counsel until they approached the exit.

"We need a few things, oh yes." He didn't bother to listen for sounds on the other side, merely pushed the door open with a groan. Alaysha was relieved to see the dank inside still being pure dank and not a light filled room with a dozen guards waiting.

"We need to get to Saxa," she said, realizing other people she loved were still in the city. She felt the weight of her father's head in her hand, the softness of Aedus's palm in the other. She told herself her father deserved his death. Still. The strange chirping her chest made told her she had always hoped for something different. She squashed the feeling and felt her heart drop when Theron shook his head.

"We can't get to her now. It's too late."

Too late now, and here she was with three powerless lives in her hands at the expense of one great, powerful life. She wanted to choke.

Theron pushed the shelves closed again to create a tight seal. To look at it, no one would know it was even there.

Without a single word, he bustled about the room, lifting vials and jars and dropping them into a leather pouch. He waved them toward a staircase that led to a further, darker, and danker tunnel.

"We do know another way." He stepped in, expecting them to follow. They filed behind him, unsure where they would end up. Alaysha pressed the others forward, taking the flank, squinting ahead in readiness.

Again, they traveled without speaking. Alaysha's relief at the silence was nearly palatable, past the taste of must and mould and old soil.

Even so, she felt the despair building and had to focus on her breathing. The tunnel had started to feel too close and confined with the others' hot breath pushing out any fresh air. She grew uncomfortably constricted, like someone sat on her chest.

They were a somber group that found the end. Alaysha dropped to her haunches in the evening light. They had been roaming the tunnels for hours and her tongue was nothing but a parched bit of dried out leather. Her legs on the other hand felt like water. She could smell her father's death.

"Do we have anything to drink?"

Theron sent a furtive glance to his sandals and the veiny toes that protruded beneath his cassock.

"Nothing, then." Alaysha let her eyelids ease closed. No water. No food. Three renegades with precious little skill, and Barruch abandoned to the Emir's stables. She tried to quell the unease that flirted with her stomach. To quiet the commotion in her mind, she took stock of what she knew, as she'd been taught those years ago, during her warrior's training. Her father was dead. So too a sister she'd not known existed until Aislin had sent her to a pile of ash. Aislin and Yuri had been at some sort of subtle warfare, both for different reasons. She didn't want to look at her father's now ripening head, but she found she couldn't stop herself from peeking, her eyes open and looking at it. It lay with its mouth open, eyes staring blindly forward.

What might this shaman want with this head anyway?

"Theron, tell me about your people."

He looked at her with curiosity at first, as though he discovered he'd been caught at something very much like telling an untruth.

"We are nearly the last of our people, oh yes."

"I assume so. You are one of Saxa's tribe, oh yes?" She tried to catch his eye even as she mocked him. "Gael told me as much."

"We were a boy when the conqueror came. How are we supposed to remember?"

She looked at him suspiciously. "But you do. Don't you old man?" Alaysha moved to stand, an unconscious move that would threaten him into speech. "What is the truth?"

He said nothing at first, but reached for Yuri's head with a covert movement, twisted something from it and then rolled the remains into the cavern.

"We've seen you collect the eyes of the unfortunate. Yes. Yes, we have. We have watched and we have studied." He held out his palms to show two round globes that he pressed toward her. "The Emir believed you were doing his bidding, finding the count of the dead."

"I was," she said, inching away from the offering. They looked like they would talk to her if she kept looking, they looked like the expressionless-within would shift into something that could tell of the shock of their death, the finality of it. She didn't want to hear that, see that, or think about that.

He shook his head. "You lie." He pressed her. "Where are the others?"

She squirmed, knowing where they were, almost all of them, lying buried in her secret place just behind her in her home. "They are hidden."

"These are part of Etlantium."

Etlantium. She knew the word. She had told it to Aislin in the village before the fire, without knowing the source of meaning. He seemed to find something useful in her expression and smiled.

"The witch has heard it. Knows it."

She shrugged. "Neither of those things is true."

"It is true," he said and his expression fell from one of suspicious query to one of near reverence. He stood and bowed so low, Alaysha's confusion swept over her like a breeze.

"Save your bows for the rightful heir of Sarum when he's rescued."

She heard Edulph chuckling behind his gag and wanted to deliver a solid kick to his ribs. Aedus had taken to creeping closer along the ground so that she rested very near to the shaman. She tugged on his sleeve.

"With Saxon gone, and Yuri dead, does that make Alaysha Emiri of Sarum?"

Theron looked to be considering the question. "Tell me of Etlantium."

What Etlantium had to do with being the ruler of Sarum, Alaysha didn't understand. "I know nothing of Etlantium."

"Nothing. The witch's nohma didn't speak of it?"

"If my nohma spoke of it, I buried the memory along with countless others." She couldn't help the coldness in her tone, or the sense of dread in her voice.

"But the witch knows the word, yes. Yes, she does."

"It's in my memory." She didn't want to say how she had pulled it out. "What does it mean? And what do my father's eyes have to do it?"

Theron dodged the question by standing as well. He inclined his head toward Edulph and Aedus. "There are always better times."

Alaysha turned her back to him. "You're right. We need to get out of here." She knew the old shaman was reluctant to speak in front of two, but it didn't mean she didn't want to hear the rest. She sighed, looking toward the mountain, knowing Barruch was still in the stables being tended to by someone else's hand. She hated having to leave him behind.

"One question before we go," she said to Theron. "Who do you think I am?"

The shaman grinned, showing his copper covered tooth. "You're either our savior or the death of us all."

CHAPTER 27

The death of us all. That rang in Alaysha's ears as they trudged through the forest. Ever mindful, she stayed at the flank end, letting the others find their way ahead of her. She knew they wouldn't get far on foot, but she was relieved to be relieved of Yuri's head. His eyes now rested in the shaman's pouch that hung from his belt. The larger bag, filled with bottles and vials, he carried in his fist. She knew the baggage was heavy for the old man, but she could not take it from him. She needed to be ready if they were set upon from the rear.

Besides, she was happy to be away from Edulph's constant babbling. That too, made no sense. She remembered a robust if not evil mind, hearty and hale. No sign of madness save that lust for power.

She watched her threesome bend beneath branches and step over fallen trees, the shaman showing a seeming affinity for the wilderness that surprised her for a man who spent so much time in the dankness of an apothecary and within the gates of a city. Both of the siblings seemed to show nothing but the smallest of focus. They were so natural in their movements that Alaysha marvelled at how easily they melted into the foliage every now and then.

Aedus stopped once at a mucky pit of rotten moss and stroked streams of mud through her hair then smeared it over her arms and legs. She looked even more like she belonged to the wild. Seeing her, even in his madness, Edulph did the same. It occurred to Alaysha that the smartest thing would be to copy them and bid Theron to do similar. Best if they could all melt into the foliage.

She imagined they all stank of stagnant water, but it was better to camouflage themselves then end up facing Yuri's defected soldiers with bare-faced vulnerability.

When night came on them, Alaysha found a spot close to a stand of trees thick with leafy boughs to insulate against the dark shelf of hill. Theron rooted about for edible plants and Aedus went in search of food and water.

Alaysha was left alone with Edulph, who sat on his haunches staring at her.

"The witch of flame could build a fire to keep us warm," he said. It was the most intelligent series of words he'd strung together since she'd seen him in the pit.

"I will drink you dry if you try anything," she said and waited to see if his expression changed. She wondered, not for the first time, why the dreamer's worm Aedus had painted on him those fortnights ago would still have him in the throes of madness. She knew the madness brought on by worm was temporary.

"Do I need to bind you?" she asked.

There was a subtle shift in his expression, so she decided on a new line of attack.

"The witch sent me to kill you, you know. To kill all of these fools."

He watched her balefully.

"When we have the earth witch, we will kill you all," she said, testing him.

She didn't expect the shrieks of terror she heard when he let loose. It so surprised her to see him thrash about, she immediately went to calm him. Before she realized it, he had his hands on her throat with his body stretched atop her, her back pinned against the ground.

His hot, stinking breath raked across her face. She tried to squirm loose.

She gulped for air and brought in nothing. She wriggled a hand loose—was it beneath her thigh?—and once free, she aimed for where she thought his eyes were. The left one went squishy beneath her thumb and still he didn't relinquish his hold. She heard him, close to her ear, whispering.

"The war will not take me. The war will not take me."

She pressed harder, the panic taking over her muscles, and the survival instinct commanding her thumb.

He shrieked again and let go. She drove at him with her head, aiming for his stomach, but contacting the hard bone of his chest. Both of them grunted in pain. He fell backwards as did she, but she retained the instinct to jump to her feet even as she hit the ground.

She leapt for him, but grabbed nothing. The bushes rustled ahead of her and he disappeared behind the waving foliage. With a curse, she sprinted into the bush after him, running hard, squinting into the darkness.

The scent of water struck her. At first, she thought the panic of losing her breath had unleashed the power without her realizing it, but then she heard the unmistakable sound of rushing stream and she knew they had turned instinctively towards the water to the west of Sarum. She halted and scanned the area, hoping for a moving branch to indicate his direction. When she heard a familiar snort and whinny, she had to blink twice to believe the shadow she saw at the bank of the river.

Barruch, standing, saddled, alone.

Dear deities, someone had thought to use him to find her. Despite every muscle wanting to rush forward, she commanded them to melt into the trees. To watch. To wait.

Heartbeats later, she relinquished that command and ran forward so fast she thought she could take to the air.

Striding forward, mountain-sized and stolidly plodding, came Gael.

And gripped in one hand by the collar of his tunic, came Edulph.

CHAPTER 28

Alaysha had no sense of propriety left in her; she didn't care what the end result would be, she wanted nothing more than to feel her mount's rump beneath her palm, and the stink of horse flesh crinkling her nose.

Gael seemed to understand that. He stood a pace away while she murmured to Barruch, who was at first wont to tuck his nose away from her, all the while stepping close enough to rub at her with his shoulders. She knew he was pleased to see her, but that he also needed to punish her for the recent neglect.

"He's a good mount," Gael said.

She looked him over, trying to assess how much damage he had taken, and noticed a long cut behind his ear. She touched her neck where the wound would be on him knowing her voice couldn't be trusted.

His regretful smile crept across his face. "Avarice," he said. "He was always a better fighter than me."

She had no idea who Avarice was, but he seemed regretful about something. He stuck his free hand against the wound and pulled it away sticky and red. "It won't stop bleeding." He gave Alaysha a hopeful look and Alaysha shook her head, knowing what he was praying for.

"No Saxa." She wished she could tell him otherwise; she looked at her feet.

He said nothing about that; his face took on the stoic expression of a fighter. He cleared his throat. "This one came through the thicket with flame on his heels." He pointed at the man he held onto.

Edulph hung his head, but Alaysha caught him peeking out from beneath his hair. She would have to make sure he was tied from now on. Mad or not, it was possible he would kill them while they slept. They would be fools to think otherwise.

Gael tied the end of the rope to Barruch's pommel so Edulph wouldn't run again and swept his hand over the mount's flank.

"He's a very good piece of horse flesh."

"I know," she finally managed, and once the words dislodged themselves she found more just behind them, jammed up like a beaver lodge holding back the river.

"How did you get out?" She started. "Has the witch left Sarum?"

Gael chuckled, holding up his hand. "She's still in Sarum as far as I know. Avarice was the last of a dozen fighters. He escorted me through the tunnels as his prisoner so I could escape. At the last, we were too much in the open, too many eyes, and I had to fight for my freedom."

He rubbed at the wound, poking at it tenderly. "I hope I gave him a quick death. He'll never forgive me otherwise."

"You killed him?"

"I had to or the witch would have. And that would have been far more painful."

"What is it like now in the city?"

"As you would expect. Citizens mill about as though nothing has happened, but the guard is smaller. Those who refused to side with the witch are cinders." He looked over the river. "There are dozens of piles of ashes."

"Any others?"

"They guard the witch, though she needs none. She puts to flame those who oppose her. The tunnels are guarded."

Alaysha considered the information and looked Edulph over. Aislin had spared this miscreant but not Yuri. She wondered if Aislin could have truly pried information from a hardened warrior like her father or whether she'd discovered he actually knew nothing and sent him to a long wished-for death.

"If Yuri told her where Yenic was, wouldn't she have sent scouts to fetch him?"

Gael followed her gaze and rested on Edulph, who sat on the ground as best he could, tied to Barruch, looking out over the river.

"She may have."

"I've seen no soldiers following us."

Gael chewed the inside of his cheek. "The only trail I saw indicated a small group. There might be only a few select assassins."

"Or we brought the assassin with us."

She caught his eye and held it.

He strode a few paces away nonchalantly and she casually followed, lowering her voice as she went.

"She may have already put scouts on their way to retrieve the wind witch, and has left Edulph to distract us. But why?"

Gael shrugged and moved closer, close enough that she could feel his shoulder against hers. "It's possible we are leading her to Yenic, yes."

She was pleased he followed her line of thinking without her having to say it out loud. "Then we can't go to him, even if we do find out where he is."

"Oh, we know where he is."

She didn't dare look at him and barely kept herself from grabbing his arm in surprise. "We do?" Her voice came out loaded with gravel.

"I do. At least we know the most likely place Bodicca would take him."

There was something strange in his voice, and Alaysha decided it must be the turmoil he would feel about her being able to rejoin Yenic. They would be lost to each other then. Once Yenic and she were reunited, Gael must've wondered where his place would be. She dared turn to him.

"Know it or not, you can't take us there. Not until we know what Aislin has planned." She expected to see relief on his features. What she saw was a kind of sorrow. "What's wrong?"

She thought Gael would avoid the question but it turned out he didn't need to. Aedus and Theron emerged from the forest, both side-by-side, both carrying armloads of bounty.

Gael left her there without further word and moved to help the old man with his burden. Alaysha watched the three of them build a small, but comfortable looking encampment with neat places to sit, and later, to sleep curled into balls which might leave indentations that, to the casual observer, might be deer beds. They had several broad leaves filled with berries and fern roots, and Aedus had even managed to find a salmon that an eagle must have dropped but not found again. The fish had dried in the sun to a near translucent fillet that she had torn into pieces and placed in the middle of the leaves.

Because Edulph refused to eat, Gael tied him to a tree far enough away from the three of them that they could speak in whispers without fear of being heard, and close enough to them that they didn't need to fear his escape.

Alaysha ate the berries and fern roots, but left the salmon. It smelled too fishy and beneath the dry translucence of the top layer of meat, worms had begun to make their way through the moister bottom flesh. She noticed neither Gael nor Aedus worried about this small compunction, but that the shaman also left his on the leaf.

No one spoke, despite the ability to do so without worry of being overheard. Alaysha watched Theron rise from his haunches to wash his hands in the river and she took the opportunity to ask a question of Gael that she still wanted to know desperately.

"Where is Yenic? You said you know where Bodicca would have taken him. Is he safe there?"

She wasn't sure he would answer, but she refused to take her eyes off his until he did. The shaman was already striding back to the fire when Gael finally spoke and he only did so when he had stood and could walk away once he delivered the message.

"If Bodicca has indeed taken him to this place, it is entirely possible they are both dead," he said, then turned and strode into the woods.

CHAPTER 29

Alaysha thought she had lost all the air in her lungs and had to work at keeping her composure while they sat around the small fire, only lit because the ample breeze lifted the flame to the air without smoke. She had a hard time focusing and could hear Edulph behind her muttering to himself. In her mind, he became everything that had gone wrong with her life over the last few moons. If not for him, she would not be on this quest. If not for him, Aislin would never have found a reason to enter Sarum. She would not have fooled Alaysha into believing she could find harmony, that she could control her power, that there was a reason for it. If not for him, she wouldn't be worried right now about whether the man she was bound to was dead or alive, and whether or not she should be trying to save him: a man who she wasn't entirely sure she could trust but whom she loved all the same.

Even if she couldn't trust Yenic, she would give Edulph's life for his. If she had that choice.

She found herself bolting to her feet and storming to the tree. She looked down at the ugly face, the broad moustache and ferret-like eyes. She imagined taking the muddy strings of his hair and pulling them so hard that he came with her as she strode across the mossy ground, over to the river, down into the water where his face would take in so much his lungs would fill with liquid and he would die. What would the fire witch do then, without her mad scout? Without her covert assassin?

With no one left to do her bidding no matter how mad or sane they were.

And she would shout at him, she would tell him how useless he was, how vile a man he would have to be to harm his own sister, to ally with a ruthless witch who would no doubt kill him when her bidding was done, so she could do whatever it was with the world that she thought she could do when she controlled the elements. How ludicrous it was for him to aid her, because surely he knew Alaysha would kill him herself in the end, pull the water from him where he stood so slowly, he would beg for the fire witch to set his heart alight.

Oh, yes, she would pull his face from the river by his hair and let him feel her feet in his stomach, her heel against his ribs. She would scream in his ear that if he had come with them only to kill them in their sleep after he'd found Yenic, then he was indeed mad; they weren't fools. They knew what he was about. Feigning madness, acting contrite and afraid of his own master. Oh, yes, they knew his master was Aislin. How could they not know?

She felt a hand on her back and a second grip on her hand, pulling at her, wrenching her fist free of something muddy and wet. She blinked and saw Aedus at her feet, knee deep in water, pulling a sputtering Edulph to his feet. She felt the frigid wetness of the river rushing about her thighs.

She blinked again and saw Theron's face and his mouth working, saying something, speaking, but her ears were too clogged with her own shouts to hear.

She dragged in a breath and found it came with a sob. Two. She grasped for the shaman, catching the edges of his cassock near the neck. "I'm death to you all, aren't I? It's all I know. It's what I do. I bring death."

She thought she would stumble against him and fall into the water, but he was strong for an old man; his legs had iron bones. He caught her and held her close to him, letting her fall against his chest. She felt his light kiss on her forehead, his voice setting her chest aflame with renewed sobs.

"No, our dear witch, not the death. Not in that way." He gripped her head, cupping her ears with his hands and twisted her so gently, she didn't realize he was whispering into her ear until she registered the words. Words so stunningly clear for once that they stopped her cold in mid sob and made her stare at him in confused astonishment.

"You are our mother goddess, dear child. Liliah herself re-fleshed."

CHAPTER 30

They had settled Edulph back against his tree, although he no longer muttered to himself, but periodically cursed at them and spit in their direction. Theron ground something from his pouch and mashed it into fern root that Aedus fed him. In moments, the cursing shifted to loud snores that competed with the mating calls of the frogs at the river bank. But for the worry of being discovered, Alaysha thought the snoring far less unnerving than the vile things the man had taken to shouting at her. Aedus seemed apologetic.

"He was never this bad," she said. "Even the Edulph who took my finger was not the Edulph I knew before all this started."

It seemed the girl had forgotten that it was Edulph who had started the troubles. "You did tell me he would bring soldiers," Alaysha reminded her and the stricken look on the girl's face made Alaysha wish she could have swallowed the comment before it escaped her mouth.

The girl looked thoughtful in the dying firelight, and Alaysha realized she was recalling the abduction by her brother's band and the savage removal of her finger. For the first time Alaysha gave real consideration to how this all might have been affecting her. To discover your older brother could be essentially ruthless had to do horrible things to a young girl's spirit. No wonder she didn't trust Yenic; she'd trusted blindly and poorly in her past.

Alaysha knew exactly how that felt.

Gael cleared his throat and reached across to the girl, something Alaysha hadn't thought of doing. "Your people are a fierce one," he said. "We can thank the deities you are on our side."

Aedus offered a tremulous smile and settled closer to the fire, reaching her hands out to it. Gael's mention of the deities brought back the shaman's whisper, one Alaysha hadn't dared to believe she'd heard. She'd tried to brush it away from her mind, but here it was, returned again. She stole a look at Theron and tried to make out whether he would offer more, but the man had retreated into his cassock and stared mindlessly into the fire. Once in a while, she could see him take the measure of the three of them and then sigh quietly as though he were working out some problem.

Alaysha found herself wondering how old he must be.

"Tell me of your people, Theron."

He looked startled at hearing his name and looked out over the fire with such longing, Alaysha felt his need to be free and roaming the wilderness. Then he gave one last glance at Aedus before he plunged into speech as though he'd been waiting for an invitation all along.

"We were taken young so our story is too long to tell, and we are old. Young ones don't want to hear all of that which has come before. But there is much to tell. Oh, yes, we have stories to tell, don't we?"

He unlaced the front of his cassock and lifted his tunic from his midriff. With a twist, he stretched toward the fire so that his ribs caught the light. Symbols danced on his skin in the shadows that played through the light it cast. Alaysha was astounded to hear her breath catch in surprise.

He looked at her and a slow smile formed on his face. "She didn't know, did she, and we surprised her, yes?" he chuckled softly. "We certainly did. But then, very few know. Those are dead now. Her blood witch, her father."

Alaysha's stomach churned on itself at mention of her aunt. "What of my nohma?"

"Her blood witch helped us find the other, didn't she? The one in hiding from us all."

Alaysha guessed the her he spoke of was herself. His speech was confusing enough to make her force him give her a clear answer for once. "Whose Arm are you?"

"She can't guess, can she?"

It was Gael who said it first, in a burst of understanding. "The earth witch."

Theron shrugged. "It is as he says."

Alaysha couldn't form the words that she needed to question him. Too many filled her mouth at the same time. Aedus was the one who asked the question they most wanted to hear. Practical Aedus.

"So where is she?"

Theron met her gaze and held it, unaffected. "An Arm is the reach of the witch. We protect her with our lives."

"So you won't tell us."

He didn't bother to shake his head, but she heard it in his voice when he spoke. "Legends speak of an old war. Our witch has the telling of it, not us, as her memory is long and her mother had the telling, and her mother before her. And her mother before. We lost our witch to the wilds in the raid when the Conqueror came, and then we lost her again finally when she was found and killed by one of her own kind."

Alaysha wanted to defend herself; she knew the conqueror he spoke of was Yuri, so it didn't take a big leap of reasoning to realize she was the killer. The shaman put up his hand to stop her from interrupting.

"It was as it was supposed to be; The Emir needed to believe the line was gone. We needed to keep the new temptress safe. And we did, yes. Yes, we did." He sounded very smug and took a moment to sigh in contentment before he addressed her with authority.

"This witch must not grieve what was not in her control."

"You set me on this path?"

"Who is this you, you accuse us of? Is it us you speak of? We let the Carrion beast discover this secret, yes. We did, didn't we? So many years ago, it took seasons upon seasons to bear fruit. Painful, painful fruit."

A flooding of memory through Alaysha's mind. "It was you. You who buried them all beneath the cairns."

He gave her a quizzical look, seeming lost in his own memories and thoroughly confused by her question. "Buried who?"

"In the mud village. All those people I killed. Someone buried the bodies beneath piles of rocks."

He grinned as though he'd just discovered a delightful surprise. "An old man. Oh, yes, I am. Even as us, we could never manage to move that much earth."

"Dear deities," she said. "It was your witch."

He lifted a scrawny shoulder. "Our witch is long lost, but she would have the ability to move rock and stone."

"So it was her daughter, then. Your new witch. She saved me," she said, realizing the full impact of what had happened in the village.

He studied her face, seeming to be searching for something more. "She is long lost to us," he said carefully.

"I know where she is."

He gave a slight incline of his head that could mean anything. She had to press him, past Aedus's hearing, past Gael sitting rapt at the exchange, so rapt, even the warrior expression of blankness had been forgotten. Past hearing things she feared; she would know, and so finally understand that thing she'd wanted to know since she'd met Yenic at the oasis.

"Who am I to you?"

Instead of answering, he sought to hold her gaze. She could feel his eyes on her in the firelight, holding her so intimately, he might have had his arms around her. "Shall I sing to you of Etlantium, Little One?"

The phrase was so familiar, so resonant, that Alaysha could feel it deep in her chest, welling within her like a river swelling. Images of her nohma fleeted through her mind so quickly she didn't have time to concentrate on any one, but the emotions that carried them filled her, emptied her, and filled her again until she could easily run back through each one of the times she had heard those words spoken. In just that way. With just the same cadence. She could hear the squall of her own cries coming back to her from a room that smelled of cinnamon and lavender and wild onion. She could taste goat's milk, and honey and the sweetness of clover, feel the roughness of homespun flax on her tongue.

"Tell me of Etlantium," she heard herself saying almost as though her words were coming from such a deep place within her that she could barely form the words.

She heard him chuckle and looked at him in surprise.

"What?" he asked with a tease. "What is there to say that you don't remember, Little One, for your memory is long and the tale is so very simple?"

Four temptresses, one large garden of children planted in refuge until twin gods could decide who had the right to rule. Etlantium in balance, so the songs say, its temptresses set to flesh the dead over and over until the war was won, and the children could once again return to their maker, their mother, the rightful ruler of Greater Etlantium.

"A hymn, not so much a song," she said and Theron nodded.

"All true, so our legends say, so says our witch. Or so our witch is taught by her mother and hers and hers and hers. And yet there is more, oh yes, there is. And our witch knows the telling of it, doesn't she? Of how to reflesh the dead, how to use the power to control the balance. These witches, these foul temptresses have all bastardized the power, abused it, forgotten what it is for, but we remember because our witch remembers.

"And in the tunnels, somewhere in the mountain, lost for generations of seasons, lies the full secret. Who is the goddess and who is the god." He looked off into the star-clad sky. "And one day we will find Etlantium again if the brother Hel does not find Liliah first."

Alaysha couldn't bear to break his sacred silence, but she so terribly wanted to know. She so badly wanted to hear him say it so she could be sure she'd heard it.

"And where is Liliah?"

He levelled her with a blank stare. "We believe she is one of the temptresses."

"And Hel?"

"He is also a witch."

"Aislin," Alaysha murmured, realizing it suddenly.

"My apologies, Witch," Theron murmured. "At first we feared it was the witch in front of us, yes, we did. But we know now that she is not. We also know Hel remembers who he is. The gift of long memory gives him power to remember his waiting life. And so he waited and searched with each fleshing he had to endure, knowing some day they would be here together.

"And his sister god has come; he just didn't know the disguise. She was wise enough to keep it from everyone... even herself."

Alaysha was so lost in the words, she wasn't aware Theron had stopped speaking until she heard the low timbre of Gael's voice. "Didn't know?" He stressed the past tense and Alaysha picked up on it.

"Indeed; didn't," Theron said to Gael. "But now he does. He knows she is a witch, but doesn't know which." He smiled at his awkward pun.

"What will he do when he finds her, this Liliah god?" Gael asked.

Theron made a small moue. "He would know these things if his father was not such a bully. The youngest of our witch's fourteen children, he should know, should have taught him. Yes, he should have."

"He didn't," Gael said shortly unable to defend himself over the negligence of a violent father years after his death. "So what will this Hel god do? I asked you. What will he do when he finds her?" He watched Alaysha's face as he asked the question of Theron, and she had the feeling he'd heard the shaman's words as they'd stood in the river.

"He will take from her the fleshing she has disguised herself in, and take us, all of us, her children, so they can no longer be fleshed, and he will seize Etlantium and she and her children will be no more. They will be as nothing, in nothing, of nothing. And the goddess will be no more ever."

Alaysha shivered at the timbre and soberness of his words despite the heat coming from the fire. Would it be so bad, this loss of flesh? Would it be so terrible to go back to nothing and be as though existence had never been suffered?

"Doesn't sound so bad to me," she said.

"No?" Theron asked, then chuckled mirthlessly. "Perhaps for the savages, it wouldn't be. Oh no. They would go on about their lives on this dirt and die their one death and go into the ground and never know another bliss.

"But us. We of Etlantium, we know better; yes, we do. We know what it is like to live in paradise with our goddess and drink of her wine and enjoy pleasures the like these savage men can never know."

"Do you remember those times, Theron?" She couldn't help the scorn in her tone.

This time he reached to take her hand and he squeezed it so hard she winced. "The real question is does this witch?"

It took her by surprise, that he expected her to remember such a thing and she felt herself gulping for an answer.

He let go her hand. "Never mind. We know these things, even if we don't remember. It is the witches' chore to bring us back to those places we have forgotten. And if the savage world will tear itself to pieces over the power our Liliah has bestowed upon a few women, then let them tear it; we will be as nothing anyway and so the suffering for us will be small."

Alaysha might not be fully ready to accept herself as a goddess come to the savage world, as Theron put it, and she might not be ready to accept the foolish legends of a paradise past her eyes and touch, but the world she lived in right here and now was filled with people she loved—who would be embroiled in a war no matter what the reason for fighting it.

So, if war was to come, let it. She would put her own body in defence of those she loved until she was no more.

She looked around the motley crew, from the still muddy girl to the old shaman. Gael was both pale and handsome even in the firelight and his expression said more to her than words ever could. She knew he would do all he could to protect her, down to putting his body in harm's way for her. Aedus too, would put her considerable cunning to use in her defence. Theron's knowledge was enough to arm them against the coming tide of fear.

And Yenic. Wherever it was Bodicca had taken him; indeed, if both of them still lived, where he would stand in the war against his own mother, Alaysha didn't dare imagine. Her eyes burned just thinking about him. She so wanted to trust him, so wanted to be able to rest secure in his love for her. It seemed Aedus was right; nothing was as it seemed. Her poor heart ached from it all. Best she not dwell on it. She would gain nothing but pain and distraction. And she couldn't afford to be distracted.

As for her own power, though as yet uncontrolled, she knew it was greater than Aislin's and that she was well on her way to understanding how to harness it. She recalled her time in the flood, and how she'd at least managed to bring the rain. She thought of Saxa and how she'd been able to stop the psyching before it fully did its work.

Yes. She was closer. And that could make all the difference to accepting herself the way she was.

If she and this crew could get to the other witches before Aislin did, they might be able to defeat her. Bring the world to rest. Bring her world to rest. Let her come to some peace without worry of being used and manipulated any more. That was all she wanted, really. To live without being tired of living. Let the gods hash out what they would when they would; it was of no real concern to her.

Even so, her heart felt as though it was racing in her chest, and the tendrils of a primal fear wanted to snake through her throat. She told herself to marvel at the sense of companionship she felt, a companionship she'd before cursed as a burden and dreaded because it brought her suffering, because now she realized those things were the greatest blessing she could have.

She thought of her nohma and felt no pain for the first time since her death; she let the woman's image come as it was always meant to, the blood as a protection, as comfort, as a means to help her shoulder the burden of grief and pain too difficult to bear and knew that love could do all those things if it was allowed.

Only then did she begin to feel the sure creeping of the bare feet of hope.

The End

Continue the saga with *Bone Witch*

More from the Witches of Etlantium
(Available in Kindle and other formats)
Seeds of the Soul
Water Witch book 1
Blood Witch book 2
Bone Witch book 3
Breath Witch book 4
Theron's Tale
Sons of Alkaia:

Made in the USA
San Bernardino, CA
17 June 2018